And Then She Was Gone

Susan McBride

Mayhaven Publishing

This is a novel, a work of fiction.

Mayhaven Publishing
P O Box 557
Mahomet, IL 61853
USA

First Edition—Second Printing 2000
2 3 4 5 6 7 8 9 10
ISBN 1-878044-83-4
Library of Congress Number: 98-66690

Acknowledgments

First and foremost, many thanks to Doris Wenzel and Mayhaven Publishing for sponsoring a novel-length fiction contest which gives unrecognized writers a chance to realize their dream. In this day and age where everything is geared toward scandal and celebrity, there are few doors left open to people like me without ties or connections who have only a burning desire and a belief in ourselves to keep us going.

To my grandparents, Helen and Joe Meisel, who had faith in me from the start and who, I'm sure, pulled a few strings in Heaven to make this happen.

To my mother, Pat McBride, who has always encouraged and supported me, even when my goals seemed out of reach.

To my father, Jim McBride, for keeping a roof over my head until I could afford my own, and to my sister, Molly, for understanding.

To my fellow writers who've lent me support and sympathy: O. J. Bryson, Lynette Baughman, and Diane Cooper Gotfryd.

And to all the unknown. unpublished writers out there who are still going at it, unwilling to give up despite the odds: Hang in there. It can happen to you, too.

Chapter One

The small hand slipped out of her own, and Ellen watched the blond pigtails flopping away.

"Be careful, Carrie!" she called out, and her four-year-old paused just long enough to turn around and smile.

Then she was off, running across the grass to the swingset, her purple overalls and pink sneakers a colorful contrast to the scrubby brown grass underfoot and the stark blue sky above them.

That was one thing Ellen missed about the East—big trees that blotted out the heavens, arching over the streets like covered bridges. In this town on the outskirts of Dallas, everything seemed flat—the sky, the ground. If a treetop reached the height of a second story, it was considered towering.

Litchfield had literally been carved out of cow pasture, the over-sized houses on under-sized lots, built up as fast as construction crews could manage, one after another, each looking much like the one beside it. The same reddish brick. The same shingled roofs. Even similar brass fixtures. Tiny trees, not as high as a yardstick, depended on sprinkler-fed water to defy the East Texas landscape. Maybe in ten years, fifteen, they'd give somebody some shade.

Ellen shook her head, hands on her hips, watching Carrie play. Smiling, she breathed in deeply.

At least there was plenty of clean air, plenty of space for the kids to run around, and people who actually spent time out of their houses, walking their dogs, gardening, having barbecues for neighbors. It all had a sort of cozy atmosphere, which Ellen would have scoffed at twenty-odd years before when she was marching at protest rallies—wanting to change the world. But now, with a thirteen-year-old son and a little girl to raise, she found it soothing.

She inhaled again, filling her lungs, sticking her hands into the pockets of her windbreaker.

Her ears rang with the sounds of children, laughing, yelling. A soccer tournament was in progress in the field across the way, the crowds in the bleachers cheering on the boys and girls whose pristine uniforms would soon be stained with dirt and grass. On the surrounding sidewalks, older kids sailed past on rollerblades and skateboards, others on mopeds braced against the wind.

Jake was somewhere around, she knew, riding that mountain bike he loved so much. She wished he'd wear a helmet, the way he handled the thing, always jumping up curbs and running with the devil.

Not a bad place to be on a Saturday, she decided, wishing that Tom hadn't been on call at the hospital as he seemed to be so often.

She turned her face into the breeze, letting the soft air brush the hair from her cheeks. Briefly, she closed her eyes, feeling settled in a way she hadn't in a long while. She needed this. Deserved it. Especially after the way they'd had to leave Connecticut....

"Mommy! Mommy!"

At the sound of her daughter's high-pitched squeal, Ellen stood up, shading her eyes with her hand, glancing over at the swingset to see Carrie waving at her.

"Look, Mommy, look!"

Carrie was standing on the flat wooden seat, her fingers wrapped around the chains, bending her knees and leaning forward to try to make herself sway.

Ellen's stomach lurched.

She started running, calling out as she did, "Carrie, no, honey, down...sit down."

She got to her quickly and caught her around the waist. Her heart pounded as visions of her little girl falling raced through her head, and she'd already gone through enough blood and stitches with Jake to last her a lifetime.

"But Mommy," Carrie was saying, "All the big girls stand up."

"You're not big yet, Carrie," she told her as she set her on the ground and crouched beside her to adjust the purple straps of her overalls that had slipped off her shoulders. "And even when you are, I'm not sure I want you standing on the swings. You got that?"

"But Mommy..."

"You got that?"

She nodded, each jerk of her little chin defiant. The

7

wide blue eyes frowned, her plump pink lips pouted, and one tiny finger reached up to twirl the tip of a pigtail.

Stubborn girl, Ellen thought with a touch of pride. Just like your mom.

She touched her daughter's cheek, the skin beneath her fingers soft as nothing else. She adjusted a pink bow that had nearly come undone, Carrie wriggled free and raced off toward the jungle gym. "Watch me," she yelled as she ran. "Watch."

Ellen kept an eye on her for another few minutes, smiling and waving, before Carrie got herself involved in a game with some new playmates. Ellen headed over to the picnic tables where the mothers had gathered to talk.

She said hello to the group, then slid in beside a slender woman with blond hair that ran level with her jaw.

"Saw you over there with Carrie," Barb Vincent smiled. "Brave little thing, isn't she?"

"I was already counting the stitches," Ellen said, feeling relaxed by the soft southern drawl. The Vincents lived across the street in a brick house that virtually mirrored their own, down to the Big Wheels and bike always visible on the front lawn. Barb's son was just two years older than Jake, and her daughter was the same age as Carrie.

"Where's that husband of yours? Haven't seen him around for awhile."

Ellen set her chin on her fist. "He's at the hospital, healing the sick, so he tells me. Sometimes it seems he's there more than he's home."

Barbara laughed. "And it's paying for that nice house of yours and your membership at the club and that shiny blue BMW..."

"Hey, you're supposed to be on my side."

Barb's pale hand patted hers, the diamond rings she wore glinting in the sun. "Oh, I am, hon. I am."

And Ellen knew that she was. Barb had been a one-woman welcome wagon when they'd moved in less than a year ago, and because of their kids, they'd gotten close. Barb knew how to "tell it like it is," and Ellen needed that from someone.

"Things any better?" Barb's voice was as light as if she'd asked about the weather, and Ellen felt her cheeks warm, knowing precisely what she was talking about.

"Not as good as I'd like," she answered quietly and dropped her gaze to her hands, toying with her wedding band.

Barb leaned closer. "Sugar, you don't have to tell me. It comes with bein' old married folk."

"I guess you're right."

"'Course, I am."

Ellen heard a whistle and glanced over toward the soccer games. The day was beautiful for February. Back in Greenwich they would be buried under six inches of snow.

"Any more trouble with Jake?"

She sighed, watching a child a little bigger than Carrie bounce a black-and-white ball off his head. "I think teenagers were put on Earth to drive their mothers insane," she said, avoiding a direct answer.

"Only they think it's us who're makin' them crazy."

Ellen shook her head. "I don't see how he can play his stereo so loud. My God, it makes the house shake."

"And you never turned up the Stones so that your mama told you you'd ruin your hearin'?"

"It was Cream." She pressed a hand to her heart and

said with a sigh, "Eric Clapton."

Barb wiggled a finger. "What comes around..."

"...goes around," she finished. "I know. I know."

"He'll come into his own someday."

"And that's supposed to make me feel better?" Ellen asked. They laughed aloud.

They sat there, chatting, gossiping, until the other mothers were gone, and the soccer games across the park had ended, the teams packing up their equipment.

The sun shifted behind a cloud, and a chill settled in. Ellen shivered, zipping up her windbreaker. She checked her watch. It was time to gather up Carrie and get back to the house. She had to put dinner on, or rather zap it in the microwave.

The noises on the playground were fewer now. The too-blue sky was streaked with pink, the sun sinking nearer the horizon.

A child on the swingset swam through the air, back and forth, kicking his legs to go higher and higher. The chains squealed with the motion.

Ellen looked around.

Several children still clambered about like monkeys on the jungle gym, but none in pink shoes and purple overalls.

Where had Carrie wandered off to?

She brushed back dark hair the wind blew into her eyes, its breath cool against her skin. She reminded herself how Carrie was always running off, making new friends, petting someone's dog, pulling dandelions from the ground. She couldn't seem to sit still.

"Carrie!" she shouted as she started across the playground, slowly at first, circling the swingset, the slide, the see-saws, and the bright yellow wheel that spun around.

"Carrie!" She fought a rising panic.

She started toward the soccer field, looking at the faces of those who still lingered about, peering into the windows of cars still parked along the curb, but there was no sign of her.

"Carrie!"

She covered the playground again, crossed the street, and jogged up the sidewalk, heart pumping, her breathing coming hard.

She stopped people, neighbors she knew and some she didn't, asked if they'd seen her little girl. But they'd all seen so many little girls today no one was sure if they'd seen Carrie.

She ran home, fairly flying the two blocks. Fumbling with the key in the lock, she finally pushed inside, going from room to room, from the garage to the backyard and even into Tom's workshop.

The house remained quiet, save for her own raised voice, her frantic footsteps.

Jake was still gone. Tom wasn't there.

And neither was Carrie.

She picked up the phone and dialed one number after another, calling everyone she could think of, women she'd seen throughout the day, anyone who Carrie might've left with, without telling her—which she wasn't supposed to do. How many times had she told her not to go off on her own—that she had to ask Mommy first?

No one had taken Carrie home with them, though all promised to keep an eye out for her.

Ellen ran back to the park, so out of breath her lungs

11

ached, calling out until her voice was hoarse, searching the playground again and again, going to doors of neighboring houses and knocking, knocking, knocking, until darkness fell around her and the streetlamps glowed orange.

The gray of dusk surrounding her, she stood in the midst of the empty field, turning around and around, shouting Carrie's name and shaking with fear.

Her baby was gone.

Carrie was gone.

Chapter Two

The child squealed, hanging for a split second in the air, before falling, small arms stretched out like wings without feathers.

"Gotcha!" Able hands scooped him up, the little boy giggling as he was caught and drawn securely against the sturdy chest.

"Again, again," the small voice cried from the safety of his father's shoulder.

"That's enough, the both of you." Terry Fitzhugh walked into the living room holding two mugs of coffee trailing steam. She paused long enough to give her red-headed husband a stern look. "You want him throwing up all over you? It's time for bed. Think you can tuck him in all by yourself?"

David rubbed his nose against his boy's. "C'mon, kid, we're being banished to the upstairs." He brought the child over to Terry for a kiss. Then he paused before the couch. "Say goodnight to Maggie, Andrew."

"'Night," the child whispered, curling his fingers in a wave.

"Goodnight," Maggie said.

"Sometimes I wonder who's the bigger baby," Terry said, pushing a mug into Maggie's hands, then settling down on the sofa beside her. "Hell, I counsel children everyday. You think I would've known better than to marry a man who never grew up."

Maggie laughed, cradling the warm cup in her hands, breathing in the coffee-scented steam. "David's a good guy, Terry. I'd say you're lucky."

"There are other good ones out there, you know."

"Last I heard, the Pope's unavailable. He's too old for me besides."

Terry shook her head, smiling. "C'mon, Maggie. Don't give up on men just because half the guys you meet on the job think women should be barefoot and pregnant, and the other half are killers and rapists."

"Jesus," Maggie said and rolled her eyes.

It was more like she spent her shift with shoplifters and petty thieves. Litchfield was hardly a hotbed of crime, despite being situated less than twenty miles beyond the Dallas city limits. Maggie had put in more than five years with the DPD after college, dealing with a department full of male chauvinist pigs, handling low priority cases, having partners pass her around like a bubblegum trading card because no one wanted a pair of breasts backing them up. Still, she'd toughed it out, doing her job and doing it well, getting booted up from blue uniform patrol to detective at twenty-seven, just before she'd transferred out to Litchfield. Close as it was, it seemed a million miles away in some respects. She'd seen too many gangs in south and west Dallas, too many babies with guns in their hands; too many school-aged kids with bullet holes in their heads, blown away because of the colors they wore or their hundred dollar pair of Nikes.

That's how she'd met Terry, who'd been working with the city, then, herself, trying to dig into the psyches of children who suffered abuse or inflicted it. Now Terry had a private practice in North Dallas, a neat two-story house in Litchfield, and a husband and kid. Had he still lived, Norman Rockwell would've drawn them.

Maggie brought the mug up to her lips, gulping down a sip of coffee that scalded her tongue and her throat on its way to her belly.

"I'd say you've got it made," she remarked quietly, briefly meeting Terry's eyes before glancing away toward the doorway where David and the baby had disappeared. She imagined him reading Andrew a bedtime story, the lights low, the scent of talcum powder caught within the soft folds of the blanket that covered him. Her chest tightened suddenly. That was how it should be, not how it always was.

"All right. What is it?" Terry put her cup on the table and leaned toward Maggie, resting a hand on her arm.

Maggie turned to find herself being studied as she imagined Terry would one of her patients. Concerned brown eyes watched her from beneath close-cropped black hair that framed her pale face like fringe.

"I feel like I should lay down for this," she said, but Terry didn't laugh.

"I'm your friend, remember?"

15

A friend who happened to pick people's brains for a living and knew just how to ask those questions that made Maggie prickle up like a porcupine.

"Is it your mother?"

Maggie closed her eyes. "Terry..."

"Well, you were kind of shaken up after you met with her doctor awhile back."

"I really don't want to get into it."

Terry never gave up so easily as that. She was paid eighty bucks an hour to pry. "I realize you and your mom aren't exactly close. But it still has to be hard on you, what with her being sick..."

"She hasn't got cancer, for God's sake," Maggie cut her off, wanting to get off the subject and quickly. Her feelings for Momma were too hard to deal with. "She forgets things is all."

"It'll get worse. You know that."

Maggie knew all right. Momma's doctor had given her a crash course in Alzheimer's 101. That was the presumptive diagnosis, anyhow.

"If there's anything I can do..."

Maggie stared into her coffee.

Terry squeezed Maggie's arm, her voice suddenly softer. "You don't have to play the tough cop with me, all right? I worry about you, how you're handling things. I realize you don't like people butting into your life, but I'm here if you ever need me."

When Maggie didn't respond, Terry sighed, drawing her hand away. "God, you're impossible."

Maggie's pager went off, and she reached toward the coffee table to retrieve it. She checked the sequence of digits that scrolled across the tiny screen.

"Saved by the beeper," Terry muttered and pushed up off the couch. She crossed the room, slipping through an opened archway into the kitchen.

Maggie clipped her pager to her belt and reached for the telephone on the nearest end table. Catching it between her ear and jaw, she dialed her partner's cell phone.

"It's Ryan," she said when she heard his familiar bark. "What's up?"

"Hate to spoil your fun, but your break's over," John Phillips informed her. "Dispatcher sent out a patrol car an hour ago to one of them fancy neighborhoods you can't afford on a cop's salary."

She waited for him to finish.

"A kid's missing. Little girl. Been gone since four o'clock."

Maggie looked at her wristwatch. It was nearly eight now.

"I'm at the parents' house. Ah, Christ...it's fifteen ninety-six Sparrow just past Woodlawn. Get your ass over here pronto."

Chapter Three

Her headlamps cutting through the pitch, Maggie glanced around her as she drove, glancing at empty fields with construction signs announcing new subdivisions soon to come, at houses that followed after, neatly set side-by-side, gas lamps casting pale light across well-tended lawns.

She frowned, going over the bits and pieces Phillips had told her on the phone. A four-year-old named Carrie Spencer was missing. Her mother had taken her to the park for the afternoon, and the child had vanished into thin air.

Litchfield was considered a safe place to live. The overpasses didn't yet have graffiti. Parks were clean. Schools didn't need metal detectors or off-duty police patrol. There hadn't been a single homicide in the past two years since Maggie had been on the force, which had only two dozen sworn officers and trained citizens on its payroll, hardly as big as some girl scout troops.

But that didn't mean that something couldn't happen

here. Texas was a state full of little towns where murder was just something read about in the papers until a quiet Luby's cafeteria became a shooting gallery for a lunatic with an automatic weapon. Then it was all too real.

She slowed the car as she passed the park, its grounds dimly-lit. Groups of picnic tables sat beneath trees hardly tall enough to shade them. Jungle gyms, swingsets and teeter-totters crowded a playground partially carpeted with cedar chips.

Small groups of people wandered around, flashlights dancing in the dark like fireflies. A patrol car eased by her, cruising the perimeter.

Maggie looked away from the park to check the street signs. She took a right on Sparrow, driving alongside sidewalks that, like the park, were filled with people. Houses were lit up like it was Christmas.

The two-story brick home halfway up Sparrow was easy enough to find. Men, women, and children congregated on the front lawn. A pair of blue-and-whites sat at the curb, the battered Ford that Phillips drove right behind them.

Maggie pulled up as close as she could, shutting off her lights and grabbing up her oversized bag.

Her stomach knotted as she got out of the car and headed toward the house. Faces shadowed by the porch light turned her way, voices hushed. No one stopped her with questions.

She rang the bell and had hardly taken a breath when the door swung open.

A uniformed officer stood in the glow of the foyer, her dark hair pulled off her wide brow and into a neat ponytail. Charlotte Ramsey nodded at Maggie, then quickly stepped aside so she could enter.

"Follow me," she said. "Detective Phillips is with Mrs. Spencer and a family friend."

"What about the father?"

"He's out looking for the girl, I think," Ramsey said. There was pity in her face.

Maggie nodded, holding off on any further questions.

Ramsey led her through the marble-tiled foyer, up a carpeted hallway with gently-lit watercolors and oil paintings, and finally into a den with bookcases running from wall to wall.

Ramsey closed the door behind her.

Phillips stood as she entered, and Maggie worked her way toward him, circling an enormous leather couch and a coffee table filled with photographs. His pale eyes watched her from a face tanned and wrinkled like broken-in leather. Phillips didn't believe in SPF's of any number and had had enough skin cancers removed to prove it. What little hair remained atop his head looked wind-tossed, though he'd obviously made some attempt to smooth it. His striped tie was loosened, his navy jacket unbuttoned to allow the softness of his belly to hang freely over his belt buckle without further restraint.

Although he looked like time had worn him down, he was only in his mid-forties and as good a cop as they made. Thorough and dogged, he'd never once, since they'd been paired together, made any reference to her gender. Something that had earned him Maggie's respect, if not her gratitude. He'd transferred from Fort Worth to a fledgling Litchfield force ten years before. He had two children, little girls, and he'd said that if he wanted to stick around to see them grow up, he figured Litchfield was the place to do it.

"Detective Ryan, glad you could make it so quickly."

He waited till Maggie was at his side to incline his head toward a pair of ladies seated on the couch so close to one another they could've been joined at the hip. A blonde with a pageboy had her arm around the shoulders of a short-haired brunette who dabbed at her eyes with a raggedy tissue.

"Ellen Spencer is the missing girl's mother," Phillips said in lowered tones. She wore a silk jogging suit Maggie had seen at Macy's in one of the pricier departments. "That's her neighbor from across the street, Barbara Vincent." The blonde was bone thin, with sharp features, ones Maggie had always thought of as Texas-grown.

"Here." Phillips passed her a photograph of a girl's smiling face, the round cheeks flushed, the eyes as clear a blue as the sky in the background. Her sand-colored hair was tied in pigtails with ribbons. She looked happy, like every child should be at four years old. Happy and safe.

"Cute, isn't she?" His jaw was set, and Maggie realized he was probably thinking of his own girls, maybe even realizing that this could be one of them. The world was so crazy.

"You meet Mr. Spencer?" she asked him, shifting her eyes back to the picture.

Phillips shook his head. "Apparently, he took off like a bat out of hell before a car was even dispatched, and, as far as I know, he's still out there, looking. He's a doctor, an internist. Been on call all day at Methodist Hospital, Mrs. Spencer said. Claims she'd paged him for nearly an hour before he showed up. He had left the hospital, but had never phoned home."

He must be frantic, Maggie thought, returning here to find out that his little girl was missing.

21

"There's a boy, too," Phillips went on. "Name's Jake. He's thirteen, she says. Been riding his bike all afternoon, and he hasn't come home yet."

"You think Carrie could be with him?"

"We've got a couple cars out looking for him as well as the girl. They're going through the house and the yard now for good measure. McMartin's setting things up in the guest room, handling the phone."

"Any relatives in the area?" she asked.

"Dr. Spencer's parents are both deceased," Phillips told her, consulting his notepad. "Her folks are up East in Connecticut."

Maggie stared at the photograph of the smiling child, a sinking feeling in her gut. Things weren't sounding good, she realized. Not good at all. "What else do you know?" She slipped the photograph into her coat pocket.

He half-smiled. "Same as you now."

"For God's sake." The irate voice belonged to the blonde whose cool blue gaze targeted Maggie. "Why don't you all do something 'stead of standin' around whispering?" She wiggled manicured fingers at them, the tips painted a shell pink. "Can't you put out one of those all-points bulletins, or whatever the hell it's called?"

"We've done that, ma'am," Phillips assured her, settling into his chair. Maggie sat down on a chair she pulled up beside him. "We've also faxed Carrie's picture to neighboring juris-dictions, and we're in touch with the National Center for Missing and Exploited Children, so if anything turns up on her, we'll find out."

Ellen Spencer nodded, the movement stiff, the cords in

her neck drawn tight. Maggie felt something like a voyeur, glimpsing such private pain, and she busied herself, digging inside her bulky purse, feeling the .38 as she rifled through its contents, in search of her notebook and pen.

She looked up to find Mrs. Spencer watching her. This time, Maggie did not turn away. The woman's strain was apparent in the tension that tugged at her mouth and her eyes. But the tilt of her chin told Maggie she had not given up. Maggie had seen that look before in many a mother's face, and still it got to her.

Maggie shifted in her seat, clearing her throat, pushing down her own emotions.

"Could you tell me what happened, Mrs. Spencer?" she asked, holding her pen poised above the spiral notebook. "Think hard, will you please, and describe anything you remember. Who was at the park. Everything."

Barbara Vincent sniffed, laying a hand on Ellen's shoulder. "She already told the whole story to those police officers who showed up first. We gave them lists of everyone we know and enough pictures of Carrie to fill a scrapbook."

Phillips cut her off, though he didn't raise his voice. "If you don't mind, Mrs. Vincent, we'd like to hear it from Mrs. Spencer. There might be something additional she can remember."

Barbara Vincent pressed her mouth into a thin line, her hand still resting on Ellen's arm.

"Mrs. Spencer?" Maggie urged softly.

Ellen sighed and pushed the tissue to her eyes with trembling fingers. "It was like any other Saturday. I caught up on housework, and Carrie played upstairs. Sometime in the afternoon, maybe two o'clock, she started getting antsy. The weather was so nice, I couldn't blame her. Jake had taken off after lunch on his bike, and Tom had left for the hospital at some god awful hour of the morning." Her chin quivered. "I wanted some fresh air myself, so I took Carrie to the park."

She hesitated, drawing the tissue again to her eyes. Barbara Vincent squeezed her shoulder.

Maggie pressed gently. "Did you walk to the park, Mrs. Spencer? I noticed it's only a couple blocks away."

"Yes, we walked."

"So Carrie knew the way?"

Her eyes flickered. "I guess she does. We'd gone so often before, and Carrie's so bright." The narrow brow wrinkled up beneath the short dark hair, and Ellen's gaze fell to her lap, to the Kleenex she'd begun shredding into tiny white flakes. "The last I remember, she was on the jungle gym. She was laughing...she looked so happy, I didn't think anything..." she stopped and swallowed. Maggie could see she was fighting to keep herself from falling apart.

"I sat with Barb at the picnic table," she continued slowly. "I guess I lost track of time, until it started getting dark." She grew more agitated, hands moving, feet shifting. "I couldn't find her...I looked all over for her...for her purple overalls and pink tee-shirt. Carrie always liked bright colors." She paused and turned to Barbara Vincent. "Oh, God, she didn't have a sweater on. She'll be cold. It's supposed to get near to freezing." She fixed her tear-filled eyes on Maggie. "How could it have happened? She was there one minute, and then she was gone."

Maggie leaned closer. "Did you see anyone who

seemed out of place?"

Ellen shook her head.

"Did Carrie know not to talk to strangers?"

"Yes...yes, we went over it a thousand times with her, just like we did with Jake." She covered her face with her hands. "Please just find her," she cried. "Please bring my baby home."

"We're doing all we can, Mrs. Spencer," Phillips said, the calm in his voice almost convincing. "We've got our patrol cars out looking, and we're getting her photo out to the media. We'll need to monitor your phones in case there's a ransom."

"Oh, God." Ellen drew away her hands and closed her eyes. Still, the tears slipped down her cheeks. Barbara Vincent held her as she moaned aloud, "My baby, my baby."

The door to the den came open, and Maggie glanced up at Charlotte Ramsey. "Detectives," she said, eyes shifting from Maggie to Phillips then back again. "Sorry to interrupt, but Rameriz has something for you in the kitchen."

He paced the floor, hands in his pockets.

Jake, Maggie knew instantly.

Phillips had said he was thirteen, but, somehow, Maggie thought he looked younger. He was taller than her own five and a half feet, though, slim and gangly, at that awkward stage between boy and man that made her think of a bumper sticker she'd once seen that read, "Be patient, God isn't finished with me yet." His hair hung down on either side of his face like dishwater-colored curtains parted just enough for Maggie to glimpse the hostile look in his eyes.

25

Jorge Rameriz, one of their uniformed officers, pushed away from the canary-colored cabinets he'd been leaning against, his arms crossed.

"Detectives," he said as they approached him. His dark eyes held an impatience that Maggie bet had everything to do with the teenager who'd retreated to the corner of the room, glaring at them with contempt. "A patrol car stopped him about two miles away from here. Kid said he was on his way home, but they put his bike in the trunk and gave him a ride to make sure he arrived safe and sound."

Jake scowled, sinking his chin into the banded collar of his black leather jacket. It enveloped his thin chest and long arms, and was covered with a fine layer of dust. His black ankle-high sneakers were muddied. The laces on the left shoe were untied and dragged on the floor, gray with dirt. There was a smudge on his chin, dirt on his hands. His dishevelment was a stark contrast to the tidiness of the kitchen where everything appeared to be exactly where it belonged.

"You need me to stay?" Rameriz asked, eyeing Jake as if he were a rabid dog.

"No, thanks," Maggie told him. "We'll take it from here."

He gave a nod, then sauntered out of the room.

Phillips pulled back a chair from the table and sunk into it, leaning forward. "You want to sit down, son?" he said in Jake's direction.

Jake muttered something under his breath. Maggie caught some of the more colorful words. She crossed her arms and leaned her hip against the counter near where Rameriz had stood.

"C'mon, Jake," she said, watching him huddle in the corner, his back against the wall. "We need you to help us. Your sister, she disappeared from the park this afternoon..."

"I know already," he snapped, lifting his chin and meeting Maggie's eyes for an instant. "The cops who chased me down and threw my ass in their car told me she was missing."

Maggie glanced at Phillips. His mouth twitched, but he didn't say anything. She'd bet her life he was wishing he could take the boy over his knees and give him a good whipping, or maybe something worse. But, whatever he was thinking, he hid it well. His leathery face appeared impassive as he settled back in the chair, his arms folded over his chest, his posture sending the signal to Maggie that Jake was all hers. As if she wanted him.

She turned her attention back to the teenager. He walked over to the counter that jutted out on the other side of the kitchen table and pulled open a drawer. He removed a carving knife and began to fiddle with it, touching the tip of the blade to his skin.

"You were out awfully late..."

"It's Saturday, and, besides, I don't have a damned curfew," he growled, his head down, turning the knife over and over in his palm.

"Did you see Carrie today?"

"They asked me that already. Christ!" He reared his head and stared at her, his features contorting with anger. He raised the knife, punctuating each word with a stab at the air. "Like I told the other cops, I'm not her keeper. She's a goddamned pest, that's what she is, and, if I can help it, I stay the hell away from her, okay?"

27

Phillips shifted in the chair, the wooden legs creaking, but still he didn't speak.

Jake was breathing hard, his shoulders rising and falling beneath the leather jacket, the knife still uplifted.

"Would you please put that down?" Maggie said evenly.

Jake's cheeks reddened as he dropped the knife into the drawer, promptly slamming it shut. The utensils inside rattled emphatically.

Maggie took a step nearer him. "We need your help, Jake. Carrie's been gone for nearly four hours and it's cold outside. If you saw her today, if you know anything...."

"I don't," he said, but he wasn't shouting anymore. He pushed at his hair, tucking the lank strands behind his ears. "And, besides, if she's stupid enough to get herself lost, it's not my problem anyway."

God, Maggie thought, but Terry would surely have a field day with this one.

"I'm sure you don't mean that," she said softly, though she wasn't certain she didn't believe him.

Jake didn't respond. He turned away and started to pick at a callus on the palm of his filthy hands.

"You fall off your bike?" she asked. His chin came up. "You look like you took a tumble."

"Maybe I did," he mumbled, avoiding her eyes. "It happens sometimes. I do a lot of jumping, you know. Curbs and boards over at the construction sites."

"Were you with someone?"

"What if I was?" He squinted at her. "That's none of your business."

Maggie glanced over her shoulder at Phillips, thinking

this was going nowhere. The kid didn't want to talk to them, and he was doing a fine job of it. Phillips raised his eyebrows, but made no move to interject.

Maggie sighed, feeling the tension knot up in her neck and shoulders.

"Jake?"

Maggie turned at the sound of the voice.

Ellen Spencer stood at the kitchen door, looking tentative as she paused at the threshold. Her face paled at the sight of her son. "Jake? Oh, God, I thought I heard your voice."

She went toward him, reached out for him, but he pulled away. Suddenly, she looked around her. "Carrie? Was she with you? Carrie?"

"Shit." Jake breathed the word and ran a hand through his hair. His eyes flashed, his cheeks ruddied. "For the hundredth time, I don't know where the hell Carrie is! Jesus!" He turned on Maggie. "Just leave me alone, all right? Just leave me out of this!"

He brushed past his mother, stalking out of the room without looking back. A moment after, Maggie heard the slam of a door somewhere overhead.

Ellen made a noise like the mewling of a cat and closed her eyes, drawing her hands to her face.

Chapter Four

It was well past midnight when Maggie finally left the Spencer's house.

She drove through the dark in silence, the only noise the crackle from the police radio. She'd turned the heat on, and it was working its way up from the floorboards where it slowly warmed her feet. The temperature outside was probably closer now to freezing than to the comparably balmy sixty-eight degrees they'd hit when the sun was at its peak.

"She didn't have a sweater on...she'll be cold" the frightened voice replayed itself in Maggie's head, and she anxiously bit the inside of her lip.

Her eyes followed the gleam of the headlamps on the unfolding road, her movements on automatic pilot, her mind filled with the smiling face of a little girl.

The neighbors who'd taken their flashlights out to look for Carrie had returned to the Spencer's with apologies and shaking heads. They had not found her.

The patrol cars that swept the area had similarly struck out, turning the job over to the next shift.

Dr. Spencer had finally come home, but he wasn't much help either. Phillips left instructions with the night shift to call if anything happened—at any hour.

"We'll have better luck in the morning," Phillips had remarked to her as they'd left. Maggie reluctantly agreed with him. If Carrie hadn't turned up by first light, they'd get a massive search underway with promises of dogs from the K-9 unit and helicopters from the county police.

She eased up to a stoplight on red, turning her head as another car pulled up beside her own, announcing itself with the rumblings of a bass guitar and a souped-up motor. Two teenage boys sat in the front seat of a Jeep Wrangler jacked up on oversized truck tires. The streetlamps shined on them like a theatrical spot as they leered at her, making kissy faces and licking at the air with their tongues.

How tempted she was to pull them over and stick her shield between their eyes.

But the light turned green, and they lurched ahead, rap music fading in the distance. By forty, she thought as she moved on through the intersection, they'd be wearing *Miracle Ears* and working the night shift at Burger King. The image of it made her smile for the first time that night.

Her condominium complex was situated beside the newly-built Litchfield Country Club, though Maggie had moved in well before the adjacent land had been snapped up by investors who'd laid out an 18-hole golf course, clubhouse, pool, and tennis courts.

She pulled in front of her unit to find a red BMW settled comfortably in her parking spot.

What, she wondered, made owners of expensive cars think they had no rules and every right?

She tracked down an empty visitor's space further up the lot and eased into it, cutting off the noise of the engine and stepping out into the chill.

The quiet of the early morning enveloped her as she crossed the pavement to her door. Maggie hadn't been home since eight o'clock the previous morning, so there was no porch light to greet her. She fumbled with her keys in the darkness, finally jabbing the one that fit into the lock. With a grunt, she pushed inside, slipping the deadbolt closed behind her before dropping her purse and keys onto the hall table atop days-old mail.

She shrugged off her coat and stepped out of her loafers, flipping on lights as she cut through the living room toward the kitchen. The walls around her were a dark green, the strength of color peaceful to her, wrapping around her like a cocoon. Cherry-veneer shelves overflowed with books of every bent, and framed museum prints of Monet's Garden in Giverny lent color where the putty-hued sofa and chairs did not. There were no displayed photographs of friends and family, no mementoes from the past, which Terry called the "hotel room syndrome." But Maggie just didn't like clutter.

The refrigerator stood at the end of the narrow galley kitchen, and she hovered at its opened door. She stared at cartons of leftover Chinese takeout and foil-wrapped pizza, wrinkling up her nose at both. She ended up fixing herself a bowl of Frosted Flakes and took it back with her into the living room, sinking into the sofa, feet propped up on the coffee table.

She turned on the TV as she ate, channel-surfing until she came across an old rerun of *Perry Mason*. But the voices she heard inside her head had nothing to do with Hamilton Burger's cross-examination.

"...She was there one minute, and then she was gone...."

Carrie had disappeared in broad daylight. She was wearing purple overalls and a pink shirt and pink tennis shoes, with pink bows tied around her pigtails. Soccer games were in progress just across the field. Children swarmed the playground. Teenagers jumped the curbs on rollerblades and skateboards. Mothers clustered around nearby picnic tables to gossip.

Maggie doubted very much the girl had just wandered off, though it was still a possibility. More than likely she'd been led away. The question was by whom. Someone she knew? A stranger? Though either seemed hard enough to believe.

This was Litchfield. If there were any perverts roaming the streets, they hid their secrets well behind their Polo-shirted and Cole Haan-shod, oh-so-polished demeanors.

Her notebook was filled with observations, remarks made by neighbors she'd gotten the chance to interview, adults and kids alike who'd been at Litchfield Park, but not one admitted to seeing Carrie Spencer leave the playground, alone or otherwise.

How had so many pairs of eyes missed such a thing?

Maggie swallowed down the sugary-tasting milk that filled the bottom of her bowl, draining it. Then she dropped in her spoon and snapped off the television.

"...if she's stupid enough to get herself lost, it's not my problem anyway..."

Obviously there was no love lost between Jake and his little sister, she mused, as she took her bowl into the kitchen and deposited it in the sink.

Jake was a real sweetheart. The kind parents who could afford it usually shipped off to military school. Still, a part of her pitied him and his envy of Carrie, with whom he apparently couldn't compete.

She shut off the lights as she went to the bedroom, moving easily through the dark to the connecting bath where she remained just long enough to do her business and brush her teeth. Then she shed her clothes, dropping them into a pile, and pulling on a pair of men's flannel pajamas. She crawled into bed without setting her alarm clock, knowing she'd be awake even before the sun began to rise. She was a light sleeper. She had been since she was a child.

She turned sideways, pushing her head into a pillow that smelled of her own scent, a mix of Ivory soap, and sweat, and shampoo. Drawing the covers up to her ears, she took in a deep breath, trying to relax. But her mind was still working overtime.

She closed her eyes and tried to picture the park in the afternoon, the sky clear, the sun strong. She saw children running all about, heard their voices raised in shouts and laughter. She conjured up boys and girls in kneesocks and uniforms on the nearby soccer fields, the wooden bleachers full of parents cheering them on.

Her heartbeat quickened.

What parent these days would go to a kid's ball game of any sort without a video camera? Someone must've been shooting, had maybe even caught something they were completely unaware of. Something that might help find Carrie.

"Please find her...please bring my baby home...."

Ellen Spencer's voice played over and over in her head. Maggie recalled the raw fear in her eyes, the sense of helplessness that went along with it.

She'd met Dr. Spencer when he'd pulled up to the house, his cheeks red with cold, his leather loafers muddied. He'd settled down in a kitchen chair, kneading his hands, hardly meeting her eyes as Maggie had questioned him about Carrie, about where he'd gone when he'd been out searching for her. His answers had been brusque, making her feel as if she were there to intrude and not to help. He had not touched his wife, had barely looked at her, and Maggie had sensed his anger. She had felt Ellen Spencer's guilt as well, and knew it was eating her up. The Spencers were hardly the Brady Bunch.

The cracks they'd probably spackled over pretty well when the going wasn't tough were definitely showing.

Maggie shifted positions, lying on her stomach, hands cupping her head beneath the pillow.

Just before she drifted off, she saw Carrie's face, and in her dreams a little girl ran from someone who chased her, a shadowed figure she couldn't make out. The child fell, and a man came nearer, bending over her, large hands reaching down and holding her still, covering her mouth when she tried to scream. She couldn't breathe.

"Momma...Mommy!"

She couldn't breathe.

Maggie jerked awake.

She clutched her pillow, heart thumping.

She blinked her eyes against the darkness, breathing

hard, disoriented, telling herself it was only a dream. Just a dream.

Drawing herself into a tight ball, she tugged the covers over her head, feeling more secure hidden beneath them, trying to relax again, to forget the little girl's face in her dream.

But it was a long time before she again fell asleep.

Chapter Five

Maggie awoke before seven, her head heavy, feeling as if she'd hardly rested.

She sat up, rubbing a hand over her face, wiping sleep from eyes. Then she turned on the bedside lamp and reached for the phone. She put a call in to the station to learn that there was still no sign of Carrie Spencer. As soon as the sun came up a formal search would begin, emanating from Litchfield Park.

She took a quick shower and was toweling off when the phone rang.

Her heart raced as she made a dash for it, leaving damp footprints in the carpet. She snatched up the receiver, thinking it was Phillips, that there was some news of Carrie. But the voice on the other end of the line was not her partner's.

"Margaret?"

She stood perfectly still. Water dripped from her hair to her shoulders.

"Margaret, are you there?"

"I'm here, Momma," she said softly. "It's kind of early for you to be up, isn't it? Has Delores gotten there yet?"

"That's why I phoned you." Her voice shook. "I think Delores has been stealing."

Maggie sat down on the bed and closed her eyes. Oh, God, not again. "What's missing this time?"

"My nightgown and some underwear..."

Maggie's chest hurt. "Momma, Delores doesn't want your things. You know that...."

"Then someone else..."

"No, Momma, not someone else," Maggie said, trying hard to keep her voice down. "I think you must've misplaced them. Why don't you let Delores help you look for your stuff when she gets there."

"I want you to come, Margaret."

Maggie drew her bare legs up, holding them to her breasts. She pressed her forehead to her knees. "I can't, Momma. Not now. I'm on a case...."

The line went dead.

Her mother had hung up.

Slowly, Maggie uncurled herself, leaning over to replace the receiver. She raised her hands to push her damp hair from her face, and realized she was trembling.

Her mother was seventy years old. She'd been forty when Maggie was conceived. "An accident," Maggie had once heard her call it. They hadn't wanted children, which was why Daddy had left them when Maggie was barely older than Carrie Spencer.

Let it go, she told herself. Let it go.

But she couldn't stop shivering.

She picked up the towel from the bathroom floor where she'd dropped it and wrapped it tightly around her, looking at herself in the mirror.

Later, she thought, drawing a comb through her hair, forcing her hand to be steady, she'd deal with this later. Delores would take care of Momma as she always did. They'd find where Momma had put her underpants and nightgown, and everything would be okay until the next time.

By eight o'clock, Maggie stood on the winter-dried grass at Litchfield Park, surrounded by at least a hundred volunteers who'd heard about Carrie's disappearance. The child's picture had turned up on the late news as well as in the early editions of the papers. Vans from the local TV and radio stations were arriving every minute, cameramen and reporters spilling out the doors.

The latter were busy shoving microphones in the faces of anyone who looked official. She herself had been trapped between a pair of cameras already, responding to questions as best she could when there were no answers.

Her gaze drifted over to the jungle gym, its bars painted the colors of the rainbow, thinking that was where Ellen Spencer had last seen her little girl. She'd turned away for a few minutes to talk with Barbara Vincent, and, when she'd looked for Carrie again, the child was gone.

Sixteen hours ago, Maggie realized with a frown, knowing as more time passed, the chances of finding her alive got slimmer and slimmer.

"Hey, Ryan, over here."

She turned to see John Phillips motioning to her from where he stood with a contingent from the County Police, among them several dog handlers with a pair of jowl-faced bloodhounds straining at their leads.

"Ryan..."

"Coming!" she called back with a wave and headed in their direction.

Maggie dug into her handbag, slung across her shoulder, pulling out a plastic sack which Ellen Spencer had given her earlier. Inside it were a rosebud-print nightgown and a stuffed white bear belonging to Carrie. The dogs would need them to get the girl's scent.

Phillips had his hands stuck into the pockets of his brown coat, the belt hanging loose so that she wondered if it would no longer reach around his belly. His mouth was unsmiling, emphasizing his grim appearance.

It was getting to him, she knew. Really eating at him. He'd moved to this town to start a family, to raise his kids in a safe place, and now it didn't seem quite so safe anymore.

"You look like hell," he said as she approached, and Maggie raised her chin, trying to smile.

"So do you."

He squinted off in the distance. "It must be awful for them. Waiting. Not knowing if she's hurt, maybe lying in a ditch somewhere or worse."

It was the "or worse" part that Maggie feared most. "We'll find her," she said, and he nodded, though she realized he knew as well as she that such a promise wasn't up to them to keep.

She turned over Carrie's things to the K-9 officers, watching as the bloodhounds sniffed the items, then whined and tugged on their leads. Noses to the ground, they took off, their handlers in tow.

Maggie put a hand over her eyes to shield them from the ever-rising sun and caught sight of Sergeant Harlin Morris, or "Sarge" as he was better known around the Litchfield PD. He was a large man, like a blue-uniformed Patton, waving his big hands as he talked to a pair of men in dark pants and jackets with "FBI" stamped across their backs in white letters.

Sarge was in charge of the search and had set up a temporary command post at the nearby picnic tables. He had a map he'd drawn up this morning, dividing the neighborhood up into sections with patrol officers assigned to each. They'd go from door-to-door, until all the houses in the area had been covered. If Carrie still wasn't found, they'd expand the perimeter of the search. Maggie only hoped it could all be done before darkness fell and put a stop to their efforts.

A deafening whir filled the air, overwhelming even the murmur of voices from the gathered crowds, and Maggie lifted her gaze to see a helicopter fly by overhead.

This one looked like an official police chopper, though she'd already seen several with news-station logos hovering over the park, then swimming through the air away, above the nearby pastures where the K-9 unit was heading.

They would find her, wouldn't they?

The hair on the back of her neck prickled.

"You all right?" Phillips was watching her, his brow wrinkled up in accordion pleats.

She sighed, feeling weary, though the day had barely started. "I'll be better when we've got her."

"Think she's alive?" he asked pointblank. "I mean, do you honestly believe it? You and I both know that when a perp

41

takes a kid, if he's gonna bring her back, he usually does it the same day."

Wind blew her dark hair into her eyes, and Maggie pushed the strands away, tucking them behind her ears. "I don't want to think of that right now."

"You figure it's someone she knew?"

Maggie shrugged.

"It's just that nobody heard her scream...no one remembered seeing the kid being dragged off, kicking and fighting."

Another helicopter swept into the sky overhead, and Maggie clenched her teeth till it was gone again, till she could hear herself think. She'd been wondering the same thing. "Abductions by strangers are pretty rare, right? Though, God knows, nothing's for sure these days." She tilted her face to the sun, wishing it could warm her, but the chill she felt remained. "It could've been anyone."

She shoved her hands into her coat pockets, hunching up her shoulders, staring back toward the jungle gym, at empty swings the wind gently pushed to and fro. "Sometimes the people we trust the most turn out to be monsters."

"Back on the Fort Worth PD, we nailed a priest who'd raped about a half dozen altar boys." Phillips shook his head, making a noise of disgust. "I mean, if you can't trust a fucking priest, who can you trust?"

Maggie gave him a thin smile and reached up to pat his shoulder. "God, Phillips, and I thought I was a cynic."

The line of his mouth twitched. "You're too damned young to be cynical."

"I'm twenty-nine," she said, drawing up the collar of her coat, "which in cop years is, what, fifty-eight?"

"Which makes me eighty-eight? Jesus." He grinned. "Hell, just wait till you've been around another fifteen. That'll give you plenty to be cynical about." Abruptly, he shut up and looked over her shoulder.

Maggie turned around to see Sarge coming toward them, the FBI agents at his side, as well as a couple uniforms from the county.

He started barking at them when he was still yards apart. "Phillips, get my bullhorn from the car, would you?"

"Sure, Sarge," he answered, his gaze resting briefly on Maggie, before he left, hurrying toward the black-and-white parked at the curb.

"And Ryan..."

"Yes, sir?"

"Get the Spencers the hell away from here."

"The Spencers?" She followed his gaze to the street where a blue BMW had parked. Ellen and Tom Spencer stood beside it, trapped by the surge of reporters and cameramen who surrounded them like vultures.

"Take them home, for God's sake."

"I left them with Rameriz not ten minutes ago..."

He didn't let her finish. "Just do it, all right?"

Maggie bit her lip, knowing that to do anything else would get her into deep shit and seeing as she didn't have on wading boots, it was best to let it drop.

Phillips returned with the bullhorn, and Sarge headed toward the picnic benches. He climbed atop a near table, standing with his feet apart, his stocky build formidable in his neat-fitting uniform, silver shield at his breast. He pulled the bullhorn up to his mouth, his voice booming across the park as he laid out instructions to the volunteers.

Maggie tuned him out, weaving through the people toward the crowd of media pinning Tom and Ellen Spencer against the shiny blue Beamer.

She pushed through them, putting an end to the filming and the rapid-fire questions. "Show's over, folks," she said, settling her arm around Ellen. The woman's confusion made it easy for Maggie to guide her toward the back seat of the car, shutting her safely inside.

Tom Spencer was not so compliant. His shoulders were squared beneath his tan coat. The wind tugged at his hair, making it stand up on end. His features contorted with anger. "What the hell are you doing, Detective? We have every right to be here."

"Get in, Doctor," she told him on no uncertain terms, before she slipped into the passenger's side of the front seat and closed the door.

She heard his fists as they banged the roof and felt the car rock beneath her. Ellen was silent in the backseat, and Maggie said nothing as Tom Spencer got in. He avoided her eyes as he started up the car and put it into gear, the tires squealing on the pavement as he turned the BMW around in the street and headed home.

"We didn't mean to cause trouble."

Maggie sat across the kitchen table from Ellen. An untouched cup of coffee rested on the placemat in front of her. Tom had disappeared as soon as he'd parked the car in the driveway. He'd headed around back, to his workshop. Ellen said.

"His escape."

"We just want to find her Detective..."

"I know." There was so much sadness in Ellen Spencer's eyes that Maggie had trouble meeting her gaze. "But it was a three-ring circus even without you both there, and Sergeant Morris wanted to keep things under control."

"I'm sorry." Her voice was child-like, quiet.

"It's okay," Maggie assured her. "No damage done."

"We don't want to get in the way."

"You're not."

But Ellen still hung her head, fiddling with her own mug of coffee, and Maggie wished there was more she could say. It was Ellen's child who was missing after all. She had a right to be in the middle of things. Maggie could sense that she needed to feel she was helping. Doing something. Anything.

"Could I see Carrie's room?" Maggie asked abruptly. "I didn't get much of a chance to look around last night."

The patrol officers had given the house a thorough going-over, but Maggie had been involved with interviewing family members and neighbors, trying to piece together what had happened.

Ellen seemed confused by the request.

"It could help," Maggie said, "if I knew something more about your daughter."

Ellen stared at her for a moment with eyes ringed by soft gray shadows. Then, slowly, she rose from her chair and left the room.

Maggie followed her, crossing the foyer to the stair-case, following close behind.

The first door at the top of the stairs was wide open.

Though Ellen didn't stop there, Maggie did, pausing just long enough to see the dolls strewn about, the child-sized tables and chairs, the easel and paint set.

"That's Carrie's playroom," Ellen said from behind her, a catch in her voice, as if she were on the verge of tears with every word.

The girl had certainly not wanted for anything, and Maggie better understood Jake's envy of his sister. She would bet her life he had been told "no" often enough.

"Detective Ryan..."

"Yes?"

"Carrie's room is here."

Ellen did not go in. Instead, she remained in the doorway, her back against the frame as if that alone held her up.

Maggie's loafers sunk into the soft cream carpeting as she made a circle of the place several times just to take it all in.

The wallpaper was a floral pattern with pale pink stripes as a background, the same pink that covered the bed and its ruffled canopy. The curtains were sheer and frilly, and, when she parted them, Maggie could see the backyard below, the swingset perched upon the brownish grass. The furniture filling the room was downsized, perfect for a four-year-old child. There was the faintest smell of crayons, as if Carrie had only just put them away.

Maggie felt a coldness settle through her, a ripple of something forgotten that fought to rise up again. It was an effort to shake it away.

Across the room on the wall was a bulletin board overflowing with pictures.

She went toward it and touched her fingertips to several shots of Carrie with her mother, their cheeks pressed together, eyes crinkled, toothy smiles on their faces. There were as many photographs, if not more, of the little girl with her daddy. On his shoulders. In his arms. Atop his lap. His eyes always on her, no matter if she looked away.

"Are they close?" she asked Ellen. "Carrie and her father?"

"Yes. Very." Her voice brightened. "He's crazy about her, and Carrie thinks the world of him." A smile flickered on her mouth. "He loves to put her to bed, read her a story. 'I'm Daddy's girl,' she's always saying." The smile faded, her voice drifting. "Tom can be strong-willed, hard to take at times, but when he's with Carrie, he's a different man."

Maggie hadn't spent much time with Tom Spencer yet, only enough to get the impression that he liked to control situations and people—to possess them.

The image of him reading *Cat in the Hat* to his four-year-old daughter was one she found impossible to envision.

"Carrie meant everything to him," Ellen whispered.

"She's a beautiful child."

"Thank you."

Maggie walked over to the desk, fingering a drawing pad, pulling back the cover to reveal pages filled with a child's scribbling in colored pens. Bright blue lines made a house with an orange sun above the pointed rooftop. A stick figure girl with yellow pigtails held hands with what seemed to be a man with a hat on.

"Carrie likes to draw. She says she wants to be an artist when she grows up," Ellen volunteered and was suddenly silent, as if trying to decide whether Carrie would ever get the chance to do so.

"Would you believe," Maggie said to distract her, "that I wanted to be a dancer?"

Ellen seemed genuinely surprised. "So how did you...why did you become a police officer?"

Maggie looked down at the drawing pad, setting it aside. "I don't know," she said, though she did. She knew very well. "Why do anyone of us do what we do?"

"I think the past shapes us. It makes us who we are."

Maggie didn't answer.

"Do you think...will you find Carrie?" The uncertainty chipped at her already-fragile voice. "She is coming home?"

Maggie held onto the cream-painted chair with its pink cushion and faced Ellen. She was tempted to lie, to try to ease the woman's terror. But it wasn't something she was good at. "We'll do the best we can."

"Oh, God." Ellen put a hand to her mouth.

"You can't give up hope."

"She wouldn't have run off," Ellen said, starting to cry softly. "She wouldn't have left on her own."

"Let's go downstairs, okay?" Maggie went to her side and placed a hand on her shoulder. Ignoring the ache in her own belly, she led the woman out of Carrie's room and closed the door.

Chapter Six

Ellen flinched at the twitter of the telephone in the kitchen. The noise of it was constant and set her on edge, keeping her heart from ever slowing down its frantic beat.

She felt like a stranger in her own house, disconcerted by the ever-present people: the police in uniforms and plainclothes who seemed to have moved into her home overnight; the neighbors who stopped by with casseroles and sympathetic whispers; and friends who tried to offer her support, when Ellen was far too numb to feel.

"You all right, hon?"

She blinked, glancing up to find Barb hovering above her.

Her friend's usually coiffed blond hair was clipped back in a ponytail; her mouth was uncommonly bare, her lipstick chewed off.

Ellen felt a sudden surge of affection for her new friend. What would she have done without her to talk to all those nights when Tom was on call? All the times Jake was driving her crazy?

"I'm holding up," she lied, her voice sounding hoarse for all her crying.

Barb squeezed her shoulder. "Hang in there."

"I'm trying."

"I've got the flyers," Barb told her, slipping a Louis Vuitton leather tote from her shoulder and setting it in front of Ellen on the table. She pulled out the box from inside it, peeling off the lid to reveal a ream of white pages.

Ellen picked up the topmost one and found herself staring at her daughter's face.

"They look all right?"

Ellen nodded, tears welling in her eyes.

Carrie was laughing, her hair in pigtails as they'd been just yesterday at the playground. Above her were the words, "Missing: Carrie Spencer," and below, her description and that she was last seen Saturday afternoon at Litchfield Park.

Ellen thought, I saw her last, and fought back a fresh rush of tears. I wasn't paying attention. My God, if only I hadn't taken my eyes off her. If only I'd....

"Ellen?"

She wiped her eyes with the back of her hand.

Barb sat down beside her, leaning near so that Ellen breathed in the sweet scent of Joy perfume. "The boys said they'd take these around, ask the stores up at the strip mall to post 'em in their windows."

"Yes," Ellen whispered. "Yes."

Barb got up and went to the door that led from the kitchen. "Now, where'd they go?" She went out into the hall, calling loudly, "Tyler! You and Jake get your butts on in here!"

When she returned, she had her son Tyler with her. He greeted Ellen with a quiet, "Hello" and she tried her best to smile at him.

Jake shuffled in a minute after, his shoulders slouched, hands in his pockets. He had on yesterday's clothes, the jeans torn and muddied, his jacket dusty.

Jake ignored his mother, hiding behind his hair, looking as if he wished he were anywhere else, so that she found herself wondering what was wrong with him, what had caused him to be such an angry young man.

"You know what to do now?" Barb said as Tyler took the ream of flyers she handed him.

"Everything's cool, Mom, don't worry."

The box tucked under his arm, Tyler pulled open the door to the outside. Jake followed after him without so much as a goodbye.

Ellen watched him go, feeling uneasy. She'd slipped into his room last night and had stood there in the dark for the longest time, just listening to him breathe.

She got to her feet, moving so quickly that she caught her shoe on the chair leg and stumbled.

Barb was suddenly beside her, putting an arm around her shoulders. "Maybe you should go on upstairs and lay down for a bit."

Ellen shook her head, pulling away.

She didn't want to lay down. She couldn't rest until they found Carrie. How could anyone expect her to sleep?

"Where's Tom?" She hadn't seen him since this morning, since Detective Ryan had made them come home from the park. "Tom," she called.

She hurried out of the kitchen and through the hallway into the living room, a trio of unfamiliar faces glancing up as she walked in, staring at her, making her feel like a freak.

How long would it be like this?

She fought to catch her breath.

But the walls closed in on her, and she ran back through the house, past the ringing phone, and out the kitchen door.

She sprinted across the driveway, rounding the house, not stopping until she stood on the dried brown grass in the middle of the yard. She bent over, gasping for air, drinking it down as if it were 180-proof, potent enough to make her drunk, to make her forget.

Her gaze shifted around her, to the tiny trees that would take years to grow as high as the house, to the swingset with its red and yellow poles, and then to Tom's workshop.

A light glinted behind the smudged windowpanes.

Instinctively, she walked toward it.

The doorknob twisted at her touch, and she went in without knocking, though Tom had told her time and again not to do so. It was his space, he said. "The men's room," she'd once called it.

But she didn't have time to think of rules. She didn't have time to think at all.

He sat at the workbench, the fluorescent bulbs flickering overhead. Beyond was a closed door, the tiny darkroom he and Jake had always wanted.

His head was bent down as he studied something in his hands, toyed with it.

He hadn't, she realized, even heard her.

She went toward him, her sneakers quiet on the concrete floor. She stopped when she was standing behind him.

"Tom?"

He jumped, fumbling with whatever it was he held,
quickly shoving it in his pocket. He came off the chair and
faced her.

"For Christ's sake," he said, looking, she thought, a little guilty, "you half-scared me to death."

"I'm sorry," she told him, words she'd uttered so often
of late, so many times because she didn't know what else to say.

"Has something happened?" he asked, the glint of
annoyance gone. "Is it Carrie?"

"No." She shook her head, lacing her fingers together,
wondering if they would ever stop trembling. "I just needed...fresh air."

She saw his beeper hooked onto his belt. It seemed like
an appendage these days, like fingers and toes he couldn't do
without.

"Did you want something?" he asked her, shifting his
feet. He shoved a hand into his trouser pocket.

She stared into his face, at gray-blue eyes she used to
feel as if she'd drown in. There were lines there she hadn't
remembered, deep creases at his mouth, no doubt from strain.

How easy it had once been just to reach out and touch
him. It wasn't so long ago that he would have drawn her into
his arms without her asking, would have wanted to hold her
that way.

She felt so alone suddenly. The smell of the room—of
wood shavings and paint and those chemicals he used in the
darkroom—seemed to choke off her air.

53

What had happened to them? What had happened to those days? He had promised her things would change when they got here, had sworn to her it would be like it was again.

"I need you," she whispered, the sound of her voice raspy, clawing up from unseen depths. "Help me, Tom. Please, help me."

"My God, Ellen."

And she went to him, wrapping her arms around his chest, pressing her cheek to his shirt and breathing him in, clinging to him as if, without him, she would sink.

His arms came around her, slowly tightening, and she started to cry, not even pretending to be strong. She felt frightened and small and weak, and she wanted her daughter back.

His hands stroked her hair, but he didn't say a word, didn't tell her it would be all right, that he would fix it.

And she wondered, as the tears fell and she clung to him, if he was thinking, as she was, that it would never be all right again.

Someone knocked at the door, and Tom pulled apart, backing away.

Ellen wiped the tears from her eyes.

The door opened, and Detective Ryan peered in, her dark hair windblown around her face.

"I don't mean to intrude," she said, "but the dogs found some things in a field about two miles from the park. I know this is hard, but we need you to tell us if they're Carrie's."

Chapter Seven

Maggie set the pair of plastic bags on the coffee table in front of Tom and Ellen, handling them as if their contents were china. One held a small pink tennis shoe, and the other a bright pink hair ribbon.

"Take your time," she said, watching the play of emotions on Ellen's face as she reached to tentatively touch the bags. "It's okay," Maggie told her. "You can pick them up, just don't open them."

Phillips shifted on his feet, and Maggie thought he looked every bit as uncomfortable as the Spencers.

"Go ahead," she urged, and Ellen glanced at her husband beside her, though Tom didn't seem to notice. He sat stone-faced, his hands between his knees, brow settled in deep creases, looking away from the objects on the table.

Ellen picked up the bag with the shoe. She turned it around and around in her hands. The sunlight filtering through the half-drawn blinds shot through the clear plastic so that

Maggie saw the pink sneaker as she would a fish in a tank. Ellen reached for the one with the ribbon, turning it too, around and around, until, with a sob, she pressed them both to her breasts and closed her eyes.

"Do you recognize the shoe, Mrs. Spencer?" Maggie asked. "Is it one Carrie wore at the park yesterday afternoon?"

"Yes."

"And the ribbon. Is it hers, too?"

Ellen nodded, clutching the bags so that the plastic crackled.

"Are you sure?"

"For God's sake!" Tom came alive, glaring at Maggie. "She told you that already."

Phillips put a hand on Maggie's arm, taking this one himself. "We need her to be certain, Dr. Spencer. One hundred percent."

"Goddamn it," Tom said under his breath, his eyes on Maggie. "Goddamn it."

Ellen started rocking, moaning softly, her face so white it was nearly blue. Tears rolled down her cheeks, one after the other, as if they'd never stop. And in her arms she clutched the bags holding the shoe and the pink ribbon.

Tom patted her back, making shooshing noises that parents use to quiet kids. He pried the bags from her fingers, laying them down on the table, and Ellen turned to him, burying her face in his shoulder.

"Are you finished now?" Tom asked, his hand cradling his wife's head. Anger filled his voice. "Are you satisfied?"

Phillips turned away, heading toward the windows, poking at the blinds so they made little metallic clicks.

Maggie swallowed, trying not to let it get to her. They were doing their job, after all. It wasn't their intention to harass anyone, most especially not a mother who in all likelihood would never see her little girl again.

"We're not finished yet, Dr. Spencer," she said quietly. "Not by a long shot. This will take some time."

"You should be out there, finding my daughter."

"We're doing everything we can to locate Carrie, you must know that."

It was all Maggie could do to keep her emotions in check. She kept reminding herself what he was going through, the stress he was under, the fear that his child could be dead. But something about him got under her skin, the condescending tone of voice as if he were better than them; his defensiveness and arrogance. But no one had ever told her she'd like every victim she dealt with any more than she'd hate every perp she arrested.

"We'll keep looking for Carrie as long as it's light out. The K-9 teams are focusing in on where the shoe and ribbon were found."

In one of these countless fields throughout Litchfield, acres and acres of scrubby trees, brush, and flatlands; places where people still pastured their cows and horses, mixed with spanking new subdivisions and construction sites where even newer neighborhoods were going up.

"We're doing all we can," she said again, knowing that such a statement wouldn't mean much to them, not unless Carrie was brought back to their house, safe and sound.

Tom Spencer didn't respond. He turned away from her, focusing on his wife, lifting a hand to stroke her damp cheek, saying, "If she's hurt, I'll kill the son of a bitch who did it. I swear, I'll kill him."

The blinds behind Maggie snapped one last time, and Phillips came up beside her, shaking his head.

Maggie stood there, watching Tom hold Ellen, as Phillips retrieved the bags from the coffee table. Then he caught her by the elbow. "C'mon," he said. "Let's get out of here."

Maggie had been back at the station only long enough to take off her coat and sling it over the back of her chair, when she caught Greg Leonard watching her from over Harold Washington's shoulder.

"Damn," she thought as Leonard wound down his conversation with his partner and sauntered over toward her desk.

Leonard and Washington were an inseparable duo, though Maggie could only imagine what held them together. Washington was a quiet man who treated others with simple courtesy. Leonard's specialty was X-rated jokes that Washington incredibly responded to with laughter, and which Maggie had learned were better to ignore than to protest.

She picked up the nearest manila folder, rifling through its contents, trying hard to look busy, but Leonard obviously wasn't impressed. He planted his palms on her desk and leaned over her.

"There's a guy from the Pecan County Sheriff's department wants to talk to you."

She forced herself to smile at him, ignoring the smirk on his face. He had a scar that ran from mid-cheek to his chin.

He claimed he'd gotten knifed when he'd worked foot patrol in Arlington, but Maggie figured maybe someone who'd had enough of his foul jokes had stuck it to him.

"Thank you." She turned to reach for her phone, when she felt his hand on her arm.

"He's not on the line, Ryan. He's over there."

Leonard pointed a stubby finger toward a wooden bench near the door where a man in a khaki uniform sat quietly. She must've walked right past him when she came in.

She got up and headed over, pushing up her sleeves, reaching out a hand as he stood.

"I'm Detective Maggie Ryan," she said, as he shifted his regulation hat and a manila file folder to his left hand to free up his right. He clasped her fingers solidly, his palm slightly sweaty, letting go with a nod.

"Johnny Gilmore," he said, tapping a finger to the star at his breast. "Sheriff's Deputy, Pecan County."

The fellow didn't look old enough to buy a drink without getting carded. His face was clean-scrubbed and he wore his hair in a crewcut. Light brown freckles rode the bridge of his nose, and his smile bared slightly crooked teeth.

She beckoned him over to her desk, drawing up another chair. "So what can I do for you, Deputy Gilmore?"

From over Gilmore's shoulder, she saw Leonard and Washington watching her. There were more than the usual number of officers around, taking the overflow of calls that kept coming in and processing the videotapes and rolls of film shot at the park yesterday afternoon. Everyone else was out on the streets, looking for the missing girl.

Deputy Gilmore set his hat on the corner of her desk.

The folder he'd brought along rested on his knees. "It's about the child who disappeared..."

"Carrie," she said. "Carrie Spencer."

He nodded. "Sheriff Moody...he thought I might better come on over here and talk to one of the detectives on the case, 'cause we had a kid go missing ourselves just two weeks past in Pecan Creek."

He said "pee-*can*" just like a good ol' boy, but since he was sitting down with her, acknowledging she was in charge, Maggie figured there was hope for him yet.

He fiddled with the folder in his lap. "Little boy," he said, "just six years old. Blond, blue-eyed. Sort of looked like an angel," he added. He opened up the folder, drawing out a photograph, which he passed over to Maggie. "He was out playing in his front yard, and his mama went inside for not five minutes, she said. When she came out again, he was gone. Somebody must've rode along and snatched him just like that." He snapped his fingers.

Maggie stared at the picture, tracing the face with her fingertip.

It was amazing how much the boy looked like Carrie. The same wide blue eyes, pink cheeks. His hair was curled over his ears and reached nearly to his collar.

A shiver went through her, and she looked up at Gilmore. "What's his name?"

"Kenny Wayne," he told her, shifting in his seat. "Nobody's ever seen him again. And like I said, it was broad daylight. Sometime about two in the afternoon." He paused. "When word got out about the girl over here in Litchfield vanishing like she did, Sheriff thought there might be some connection, seeing as how they happened so close in time and all."

Maggie wondered if it could be true. Pecan Creek was barely an hour away, a small town in a flat rural county.

"We've had the state troopers assisting, trying to find the boy, but he hasn't turned up yet. Gotta figure he's more 'n likely dead. There's a whole lot of land in Pecan County...hell, in all of Texas. A million places some pervert could get rid of him without anyone ever coming across him again."

Maggie's mouth went dry, She wet her lips. "Any suspects?" she asked him.

Gilmore glanced around them, apparently distracted by the ringing phones and voices, the constant motion.

"Deputy?"

"Ma'am?" He turned to her, looking sheepish at being caught not paying attention.

"Suspects," she repeated.

He ran a finger under his collar. "Well, um, Sheriff Moody...he figured it might be the kid's father at first. They were divorced, and we thought he might've swiped his boy without letting the mama know. But the man was clear up in Missouri when it all happened. Seems he's been living with some woman there for years. Got two kids of their own."

"I see."

"Other than that...," he let the thought trail off and shrugged. "Nobody saw nothing. Nobody knows nothing." He shook his head. "Hell, you'd think everyone was deaf and dumb."

"Sometimes you hit roadblocks," she said. "It happens."

"Well, we're hoping you might help us around the roadblocks in this case."

"If there's a connection."

"Right."

"You mind if I copy the file?" she asked. Without hesitation, he handed it over.

Maggie eagerly flipped through it, though there wasn't much there, as the case was just a couple weeks old and the list of possible suspects didn't even add up to one.

She left him at her desk and went over to the copy machine. She was done in another five minutes and gave back the original file, putting her copy on the desk next to her paperwork on Carrie Spencer.

She tried to return the photograph of Kenny, but he waved her off. "We've got plenty of them, Detective. That one's yours."

"Thanks."

"Let me know if anything turns up."

Maggie promised him she would.

When he was gone, she sat back down and picked up the pictures of Kenny Wayne and Carrie Spencer, staring at them both until she had to put them down and look away for awhile. But turning away didn't keep her from thinking. Two children who looked so alike, so near in age, vanishing within two weeks of each other.

Kenny Wayne hadn't been found.

And Carrie was still out there, too.

"Hey, Ryan."

Maggie shuffled the photographs together, and glanced up to find Greg Leonard hovering over her again.

"You gonna take a nap on us, or do you want to give us

a hand going through the videotapes?"

Maggie nodded.

"Oh, and Washington's got those names you wanted." At Maggie's raised brows, he added, "You know, the teams from the YMCA playing softball yesterday? The coaches and shit. He's already faxed a copy to the FBI. They're gonna check for priors."

"Great," she told him. "Thanks."

Carrie had been missing for more than a day.

Chapter Eight

The search was called off when dusk turned to dark.

Despite the ever-ringing phones, the rise and fall of voices, an odd sort of silence pervaded the squad room at the station, a feeling of hopelessness that Maggie sensed spreading around like a flu bug.

Another day had come and gone, and they were no closer to finding Carrie Spencer. The tips that had come in had not panned out. Professed sightings of a little blond girl in places as far away as Tulsa had proven false.

Still Maggie fought not to give in to the familiar acceptance, the knowing of what undoubtedly was. She thought of Ellen Spencer, of the look in her eyes, and realized it wasn't good enough.

Phillips had taken off a half hour ago, heading home to see his wife and tuck his girls into bed.

Maggie had a half-finished Coke on her desk, pushed aside for the moment as she pored over yet another set of photographs taken at the park yesterday afternoon, endless shots of someone's children with a backdrop of blue sky and brown grass. She went over each with a magnifying glass, squinting until her vision blurred and her head ached.

Why did it seem they were running as fast as they could and getting nowhere?

She was about to get up to take a seventh-inning stretch, when her phone rang.

"Detective Ryan here."

"Maggie? It's Delores Jordon."

"Is Momma all right?" Habit kicked in, and she began to ask the same things she always did every time Delores called. "She hasn't wandered off?"

"No, honey, not that."

Maggie dropped her head into her hand. Her temples pulsed, and her empty stomach cramped. "What's going on? Did she hurt herself?"

"She got her pills mixed up, honey. You know how I put 'em out for her in those little plastic cups, all neat and labeled for each day of the week. Well, she got 'em all out of order and messed 'em up. She didn't want to tell me what she did, so she just took some of each, and her heart started beating something wild. I had to call the paramedics. I left you a message..."

"I'm sorry, Delores. Today's been real hectic."

"I hate to ask you, what with you being so busy and all, but could you come and see your momma? I think it might help to settle her down. You know how worked up she gets."

Maggie rubbed her eyes, thinking of what to say, that it wasn't a good time, that she'd have to visit with Momma another day.

"Honey?"

"I'll be there as soon as I can."

She gathered up the pictures she'd been going through, tapping them into a neat pile and sliding them back in the labeled envelope they'd come in.

She pulled on her coat and took her purse from her bottom desk drawer, passing through the security doors and out of the station.

The heat turned to high, she drove her Mazda through Litchfield and onto the freeway toward Dallas, feeling chilled despite the warm air blowing up from underfoot.

She tried to listen to the chatter on the police band, tried to keep her eye on the signs and the passing cars, but her mind drifted off to somewhere else.

Pieces of dreams and snatches of voices and feelings thumped around in her head in concert with the methodical slap of her tires on the pavement.

"Your daddy, he didn't want to be tied down, didn't want the job of raising a child, so he picked up and left me with you..."

A tremor pressed through her, a sense of being shut off, of reaching out for someone and touching nothing. Of crying out, and no one hearing.

She gripped the steering wheel hard, pushing her foot down on the gas, going faster than she should.

Exit signs swept past, and she switched lanes, swinging onto the off ramp toward the North Dallas Tollway.

She dug in her purse for enough change to toss into the waiting basket, driving through before the green light had flashed her a "Thank You."

She headed south, under concrete overpasses, drawing deeper and deeper inside herself the nearer she came, the closer she got.

She turned off on Mockingbird, slowing down as she passed older two-story houses whose ornate facades and well-kept lawns could be discerned even beneath the pale orange halos of the streetlamps. Barely three blocks further, the houses grew smaller and more neglected, the yards tiny and overgrown.

She saw Delores' old Chrysler parked out in the street and pulled up behind it, cutting off the motor.

For a minute, she sat in the car, staring out the window at the one-story white pillbox where she'd lived when Momma had remarried just six months after Daddy took off. She felt oddly detached from the place, from any real sense of living there. She didn't feel like it was home. She never had.

Drawing in a deep breath, she got out of her car and went to the door. Delores answered her knock.

"Come on inside, girl, you're shivering."

Maggie took her hand, looking into the chocolate-dark face, at short cropped hair sprinkled liberally with gray, the slim figure wrapped in an old cardigan. Delores lived nearby on Lemmon and had known Momma for at least twenty years. She was a retired school teacher with no family to care for, so she looked after Momma and wouldn't take a dime of Maggie's money for doing it.

"How is she?"

"Not good, not bad. They got her vital signs back to normal. She's just plain mad most of all—mad at herself that she can't remember like she used to—that she gets things so mixed up."

Delores locked the door behind them, putting an arm around Maggie as she led her down the hallway toward Momma's room.

The pale yellow walls were the same as they'd always been. Black-and-white photographs hung crookedly in cheap frames, grainy faces of people she couldn't remember.

There was a closed door ahead, on the other side of the only bathroom.

Maggie found herself staring in that direction until Delores shepherded her through Momma's opened doorway. The lamp on the nightstand was on, the light dim. Still, the lampshade looked yellowed, the wallpaper faded.

"Look who's here," Delores said in her molasses-warm way, taking Maggie's hand and drawing her toward the slim figure barely visible beneath the quilted spread. The face propped upon several pillows looked old and withered. The eyes, nearly hidden by folds of skin, fixed themselves on Maggie.

"Margaret?" Her voice sounded weak.

"I told you she'd come, didn't I?" Delores said, patting Maggie's shoulder, then she shuffled out of the room, leaving the Detective alone with her mother.

"How are you, Momma?" she asked, standing where she was, sticking her hands in her coat pockets. "Delores said you gave her quite a scare."

"It was an accident."

"Of course it was."

"The way Delores made such a fuss...calling the...the..."

"Paramedics," Maggie said gently.

"Good God! You would've thought the house was on fire, when it was just my heart fluttering."

"Delores did what was right..."

"You always take her side, for heaven's sake," her mother grumbled.

There was a photograph on the nightstand of her mother with a man, and another of a little girl whose eyes seemed sad despite her smile.

Maggie looked away.

"It's not fair, Margaret." Her mother kneaded the quilt with blue-veined hands. "It isn't fair that I can't get my thoughts straight. I keep forgetting words. I can't remember names."

"I know, Momma. I know." Maggie went nearer the bed, but didn't sit down on it.

She gazed upon the age-ravaged face, thinking of how vain her mother had once been about her appearance, how important it always was that she look her best, that she be attractive. And now she couldn't bathe without Delores to help her, to make sure she didn't slip or let the water run over the tub.

"I only wanted a good life," her mother was saying, rambling, "and he gave us that, didn't he, Margaret? He made us a family again."

"Yes, Momma," she answered without thinking, only realizing after what she meant.

"You had everything you needed."

"Yes."

"I wasn't a bad mother, was I?"

"You should rest," Maggie said, feeling things she didn't want to feel. "You've had a rough day. You must be tired."

"Don't leave me..."

"I won't," she said, and Momma closed her eyes, turning her face to the pillow.

Maggie stood there until she heard her snoring. Then she shut off the bedside lamp and walked out.

Chapter Nine

The sun had not yet risen when Maggie woke up the next morning. She'd had another restless night, and the lack of sleep was beginning to wear on her.

She showered and dressed, downed a glass of orange juice and a bowl of Frosted Flakes, leaving the dishes in the sink. There was frost on the window glass, so she pulled on her coat before heading outside.

The morning air chilled her to the bone, though she knew it would probably warm up considerably by lunchtime. The weather was like that in Texas, especially between winter and spring when the seasons seemed to blur. It might be near freezing at dawn and almost seventy by noon. It could be sunny one day and tornadic the next. As unpredictable as everything else in a state that sometimes seemed out of sync with the rest of the nation, a part of the Wild West that didn't want to die.

She drove the ten miles to the station by rote, her mind preoccupied. She felt as if she was about to lose control. It frightened her. Nightmares she hadn't had since she was a child shook her awake, dark images that sent her heart racing.

Carrie. She had to concentrate on finding Carrie. She'd always done her job well, no matter what else went on in her life. She couldn't let Momma, couldn't allow anything else to sidetrack her now.

She squinted into the pink sky, thinking of the shoe and ribbon found two miles from the park. There had been a small stain on the sneaker, like a spot of rust. She wondered if it was blood, and, if it was, whose it was—Carrie or her abductor?

The county crime lab was examining each for trace evidence, their equipment superior to anything used by the Litchfield PD. Maybe they'd have some results as early as this afternoon, if they were lucky. All she had to do was wait.

As uncertain as she was about everything else, at least there was something she was sure of—that Carrie had been led away. If she'd just wandered off, they would have found her by now. A four-year-old child could not have gone far on her own. Not so far that dogs and choppers and search teams on foot couldn't track her down.

Maggie pulled into an empty space in the station lot, killing the ignition and sitting there for awhile, leaning her arms and head on the steering wheel.

What about the little boy who'd gone missing in Pecan Creek? Was there a tie between that case and Carrie Spencer's disappearance? She sighed, knowing she was getting nowhere. There was still much more to do, more people to talk to, more videos to watch. She drew in a deep breath, trying to gear herself up before she left the car and headed into the station.

Phillips looked up as she walked into the squad room.

He waved at her, the phone in his hand, and she went over to his desk, hearing only his end of the conversation—a series of grunts--before he hung up.

"Hell, it's about time you got in. I've been calling your place for the past twenty minutes."

"I took my time getting here," she told him. "I had a lot of thinking to do."

He snatched his coat up from the back of his chair and pulled it on over his shoulder holster. "Let's go."

"Go where?" She'd just gotten there, for Pete's sake.

"Leonard and Washington were over to the north side following up a burglary call when it came in. So they went on over."

"What came in?" Maggie brushed her hair from her face. "Went where?" She suddenly caught on. "It's about Carrie, isn't it? Jesus, Phillips, spit it out."

He exhaled slowly, blowing air over his bottom lip. "They think they've found her, Ryan."

Maggie's heart leapt. It was over. Nearly two days, and it was over. She was alive, she had to be alive. "Where is she? Is she okay? Christ, do they have her with them? Are they bringing her back here?"

Phillips turned. His face was grim. He put a hand on her shoulder, and Maggie stared at it. "A construction worker found her, Ryan. They were off yesterday, so no one was on site, but when they came in today, somebody was tossing some trash and saw something in the dumpster."

Maggie didn't move. She didn't speak.

"It was a little girl, Ryan. She hasn't been dead long, they said. A day, maybe day and a half."

She raised her eyes to his, unable to react at first, feeling things she didn't want to feel, fears she'd worked hard to suppress. "Maybe it's not her."

He cleared his throat. "She's wearing purple overalls and a pink tee-shirt. She has on pink socks, and her hair's in pigtails, just like her mother told us."

Maggie struggled to find her voice. "Was she...?"

Phillips rubbed at his jaw. "Leonard said she was fully clothed, except for the missing shoe. They've called the county medical examiner in to do a prelim, but they'll autopsy the body so we can know for sure."

"Goddammit," she breathed the word.

"I'm sorry," he said, and she nodded grimly. He was looking pretty gray himself. Probably thinking of his little girls, thanking God it wasn't one of them.

She was thinking of a little girl, too, one she'd thought she'd buried long ago—only maybe not deep enough.

"You all right?"

She started to lie, to tell him that she was, and then she shook her head. She felt warm, sick to her stomach. "Let's get the hell over there, all right? I'll ride shotgun."

"Sure, Ryan, sure."

In truth, she didn't want to be alone, not for a second. She might start remembering otherwise.

The construction site was about five miles from Litchfield park on acres of old cow pasture scattered with overgrown grass and weeds and litter.

The dogs hadn't gotten this far, Maggie realized. There were too many other places to look, other fields, blocks of houses and strip malls.

Phillips pulled the car to a stop about half a block back. A host of cars were already there at the site, double-and triple-parked. But there was an unusual quiet, a somber mood.

Yellow crime scene tape wrapped around the lot of a half-built house, the foundation poured and the skeleton intact, with plywood walls erected, and an unfinished roof.

Maggie ducked under the tape, following Phillips along a pathway of planked wood that bridged over slightly muddied ground to where a handful of men congregated, Greg Leonard was among them, as well as several jeans-clad men with tool-belts slung across their hips. Uniformed officers held at bay other construction workers, a bevy of media who'd arrived already, and several out-and-out gawkers.

She caught a glimpse of Harold Washington, moving deliberately around the site with one of the FBI agents she'd seen at the park yesterday. Both had on plastic gloves, as did the forensics team from the county. In the Litchfield department, it was usually the detectives in charge who did all the evidence-gathering, taking scrapings, collecting fibers, and dusting for prints. The Litchfield force wasn't big enough to warrant having a lot of lab technicians on staff. But this case wasn't like any other, she realized, glancing at the camera crews and reporters hovering on the periphery.

She let her gaze wander further and spotted the brown dumpster at the side of the house-in-progress.

A crime scene photographer moved around gingerly with camera in hand. A woman with a sketchpad made drawings of the area. Several officers wearing plastic gloves sifted through the garbage. Another hovered over something on the ground. Nearby, a pair of attendants from the morgue waited with a stretcher.

She took a step closer.

A hand came down on her arm, holding her back.

She looked up at Phillips.

"You sure you're all right?" he asked.

Was she all right? The little girl she'd been looking for and thinking of the past forty-eight hours was lying just yards away from her, dead. She'd never known her, but Carrie Spencer had become as familiar to her as anyone she had ever known. She had never felt less "all right" in her life.

Maggie's chest constricted, but she nodded at him. "I did five years working out of precincts in south and west Dallas," she reminded him, as if that meant she could stomach anything. "Besides, we were called in on the case before it became everybody's property. This is ours, Phillips. I don't care who else has gotten involved."

"Hey, nobody's pulling you off," he said, the deep creases in his cheeks making his expression even more crestfallen. "It's just a team thing now."

She didn't respond. She pulled away from him, shoving her hands in her jacket pockets as she walked toward the dumpster.

The medical examiner was closing up his bag as she approached. He nodded up at her, his eyes widening behind wire-rimmed glasses.

"Well, if it isn't Maggie Ryan," he said, the slightest hint of a smile tugging at his lips. "It's been awhile," he added, and his bespectacled gaze skimmed over her, from her head to her toe, then back up again. "You're looking good."

"I've seen you look better, Mahoney," she said, and she meant it. His face was thin, drawn. His hair was a mess of tangled curls. He looked, she thought, as if he'd been dragged out of bed to come here, which he undoubtedly had been.

"So, how d'you like it out here in Disneyland? Lots of stolen golf carts? Don't you miss the smell of blood and guts?"

"Is that what it was?" Maggie said, remembering so well how he could make light of even the most gory situation. "And I always thought it was your cologne."

He laughed, pushing at his glasses with the back of his plastic-gloved hand. "Still the same old Ryan."

She gestured toward Carrie. "Mind if I take a look?"

"It's your breakfast," he said, the lopsided smile disappearing as she squatted down beside him.

There was a faint smell of something rotting, the vague odor of decaying flesh, and Maggie pressed her mouth into a tight line. She grappled to remain calm, professional.

"The temperature was near to freezing these past few nights, and low enough yesterday that it's kept her pretty well preserved."

Carrie could have been resting had her eyes not been open wide, the whites discolored, tinted brown as were her lips and nostrils. Wisps of pale, yellow hair had come loose from her pigtails and floated around her heart-shaped face. Her skin was the bloodless white of porcelain, now tinted blue by lack of oxygen. There was a purplish bruise on her brow near her right temple, scraped and speckled with dried blood.

"Someone hit her pretty good," he said, his voice matter-of-fact, though a small sigh followed. "Maybe used a board, though it could've been a brick from the looks of the

77

residue. There're plenty enough of both around."

"Is that what killed her?"

"Off the record? I'd say it's a good bet."

"It happened here then?"

"It's likely."

She looked around her, at the half-built house with its plywood walls, providing perfect seclusion. The fields around it, the other unfinished houses and empty lots where construction hadn't yet started, provided isolation on the week-ends. Had Carrie screamed, she doubted anyone would have heard.

Maggie turned her eyes on the body again. Her throat tightened. "Was she sexually assaulted?"

"The autopsy'll tell us soon enough, but there aren't any overt signs. Her clothing's undisturbed," he said, and Maggie nodded, noting the purple overalls, one strap unhooked and dangling, the pink tee-shirt beneath. On her left foot was a tiny pink sneaker, on her right, a ruffled pink sock.

Maggie stared at the paper bags that covered the dead girl's hands. "Did she struggle? Anything under her nails?"

He shrugged. "Looks like some dirt. She has a small cut on the second finger of her right hand, a little congealed blood. Can't tell much else until we get her on the table." He clicked his tongue. "What a damned shame."

It was more than a shame, Maggie thought, for a child to be killed and tossed in the dumpster like yesterday's garbage.

She curled her hands to fists, tucking in her thumbs.

How could someone have done this? Murdering a little girl, wiping away all she was, taking the pink from her cheeks, the light from her eyes, the smile from her face?

Had she felt pain? Maggie hoped not.

But she knew the answer. She was certain Carrie had been ter-rified. She only hoped it hadn't lasted long, that it was over with quickly.

"...wipe your eyes now, no use crying. It isn't going to do you any good, and won't change a thing. It won't hurt so bad the next time, I promise you that. Just hush. Remember now, hush."

"You through, Ryan?" the voice caught her off-guard, and Maggie jerked her head up.

Mahoney gestured at the pair with the stretcher. At her nod, they moved in and unzipped a body bag, lying it next to the child.

Maggie stepped aside.

The body was carefully set atop the opened tarp, her paper-bagged hands gently placed on her chest. The zipper went up with a whoosh, the tarp snapping. They set her onto the stretcher and quickly lifted, heading across a plywood path toward a waiting van.

Maggie watched them go, pressing down the bile that rose in her throat.

She heard the noise of the engine starting up, the crunch of the tires as the van slowly pulled away.

She nearly bumped into Phillips as she turned around. He was standing a few feet behind her. He didn't speak, just walked beside her as she returned to where Washington had joined Leonard who was still questioning the two men from the construction crew. There was such concern on Phillips' face that she found herself deliberately avoiding his gaze.

"You get a good look at the kid?" Leonard asked. He looked nervous. And Maggie knew he had every reason to be. They all did. There was pressure from the top to wrap this one up and quick. The mayor of Litchfield didn't like the thought of a child killer running around any more than did the chief of police or anyone else down the chain of command.

"Like you to meet someone, Ryan. This is Hank Tucker," Washington introduced one of the men wearing blue jeans, a grizzled-looking fellow in a thermal undershirt. "He found the body." He hooked a thumb at the other fellow, a tall black man in a flannel shirt. "And this here's the supervisor, Mose Johnson. They came on site this morning about six-thirty." Washington paused to check the scribbled writing on his notepad. "It was still kind of dark then, so nobody saw nothing. They were working on the brick exterior, is that right, sir?"

Both Johnson and Tucker nodded.

"Tucker here was tossing out some broken brick, when he saw what he thought was a hand." Washington's dark face screwed up thoughtfully. "That was about seven-thirty, did you say?"

Tucker cleared his throat, glancing around, his gaze resting briefly on Maggie. "Yes, sir, seven-thirty exactly."

"Did you touch her, Mr. Tucker?" Maggie asked, though the man looked at Washington first, as if to ascertain that her question was worth answering. "Did you pull the body from the dumpster?"

Tucker's adam's apple bobbed. "I didn't know if she was alive or not. Hell, I couldn't leave her there. We didn't move her much, just to the ground where she was when they came." He averted his eyes.

Leonard rubbed a hand over his jowls, the pink of the scar on his cheek standing out against the pale skin. "Shit, Ryan," he hissed at her under his breath, "the scene's a fucking mess as it is. Don't go getting pissed 'cause they pulled her out."

Maggie started to say something, but Phillip's hand came down on her shoulder, squeezing, and she let it drop.

"Was anyone working here on Saturday?" she asked, watching the exchange of glances between Tucker and Johnson.

The crew supervisor crossed his arms over his chest. "Had some men here till mid-afternoon," he said. "Only work a half-day Saturday. Overtime, you understand."

So no one was here late Saturday afternoon. Ellen Spencer last saw her daughter in the park several miles away at perhaps three p.m. The field where the lone shoe and ribbon were found was about halfway between.

Maggie listened quietly as Phillips asked a few more questions of the pair, until the men insisted they had told them everything.

Leonard flipped shut his notebook, shoving it into his overcoat pocket before ushering the construction workers toward a uniformed officer nearby.

He rubbed his hands together when he returned. "Now we can get to the nitty-gritty," he said.

Maggie asked without hesitation, "She wasn't just dumped here, was she?"

The brown of Washington's skin glistened with sweat despite the cool temperature. "We found traces of what looks like blood on the concrete, some blond hairs we think are hers."

Phillips rubbed at his jaw. "So the perp is probably a local?"

Washington nodded slowly. "It's possible."

Maggie thought it more than possible. Killers often didn't roam too far from home, sticking close to what they knew.

"Any clear footprints?" she asked.

Leonard glanced at Washington, and they both grinned. "What kind of footprints you want, Ryan? We've got 'em by the dozen. Every size and then some. And don't even ask about fingerprints, okay? 'Cuz there isn't a surface around here that'll give us any worth squat." He waved an arm at their surroundings. "Oh, and tire tracks. Hell, we've got those, too. Every fucking size you can imagine."

"Christ," she said under her breath. "Jesus Christ." This was not what she was hoping for. Getting any unsullied evidence from the scene was going to be as tough as finding a grain of truth in Leonard's bullshit.

"Her clothes weren't removed," Washington said, ticking items off his list, "She's wearing the purple overalls and pink shirt that her mother described when she reported her missing. She's got the pink socks on and a single shoe that matches the one the dogs found yesterday. Guys from trace evidence have already made the site, and now they're going through the dumpster. Maybe they'll come up with something solid we can go on."

Maggie waited for him to say more, and when he didn't, she asked, "What about a hair ribbon?"

Washington looked at Leonard, who shrugged.

82

"There was no ribbon in her hair. And only one was found yesterday."

"Like I said, Ryan, they're going through a whole shit-load of trash. Maybe it'll turn up."

Maggie shoved her hands in her pockets. "Maybe."

"The county boys are bagging and tagging everything in sight, okay?" Leonard sounded clearly irritated, as if she'd just questioned his ability—or lack of it—to secure the scene. "It's just there's a lot of people working here all the time, tramping around in big, muddy boots, driving across the ground in fucking trucks, you understand?"

Maggie stared at him.

Phillips cleared his throat. "Anything else?" he asked.

Leonard glanced at Washington. "We did find a hand-ful of roaches."

"You found bugs? I don't doubt it." Phillips shook his head.

"Not cockroaches, John," Leonard interjected. He was grinning. So was Washington. "Marijuana butts. Looks like someone used the place to smoke dope."

Phillips reddened. "What about the people who live in the subdivisions nearby? Did anyone see anything? Maybe a parked car?"

Pen in hand, Leonard gestured around them, his unbut-toned trench coat fluttering around his knees. "Hell, there aren't houses for half a mile or more. We're standing where, till a couple months ago, cows used to shit."

"Litchfield's full of kids," Maggie spoke up in her part-ner's defense. "Teenagers with rich parents who can well afford to buy them cars and mountain bikes. A place like this

83

might attract them. It's possible one of them might have seen something."

"Give me some credit, Ryan, would ya?" Leonard lifted a hand like a cop stopping traffic. "We've already got as many officers as we could knocking on doors. If anyone was hanging around and saw something, we'll find 'em." He hesitated, looking over her shoulder, and Maggie followed his gaze to the line of yellow tape and the ever-growing crowd that gathered behind it. Most of them media-types with cameras and mics at the ready. "Looks like we won't have a real hard time getting the word out, besides," Leonard added under his breath.

"Let me know what you find."

"Sure, Ryan, sure."

The wind picked up, and Maggie raised the collar on her coat. She held the hair back out of her eyes. "Have the Spencers been notified?"

Washington nodded. "A patrol car was dispatched as soon as we ID'd the girl."

Maggie's eyes became moist. She could only imagine how Ellen Spencer would react when she heard that her daughter had been murdered.

Phillips caught her by the arm. "I think we've seen enough," he said to Leonard and Washington. Then, leaning nearer Maggie, he asked, "You ready, Ryan?"

She went ahead of him, shoes clattering on the bridges of plywood as she walked away from the site, dodging under the yellow tape, picking up her stride when she realized they were being followed to the car.

She locked her door as Phillips gunned the engine, but, by then, the reporters and cameramen who'd dogged them surrounded the Ford, beating on the windows and shouting questions through the glass.

Maggie pressed her back against the vinyl seat, closing her eyes so she couldn't see them, a surge of relief sweeping through her when she felt the car start to roll beneath her, pulling away fast.

She let out a held breath when they cleared the street and the pack of wolves grew ever smaller in the rearview mirror.

She dropped her head back, defeat weighing heavy on her shoulders. "It couldn't have been worse," she whispered, "could it?"

She glanced over at Phillips. Even the granite of his jaw seemed to sag. "You think whoever did this to her had it planned?"

"I think he knew what he was doing, yes."

Maggie sighed and turned to stare out the window, squinting at the houses and fields they passed, not seeing anything but Carrie's face, hearing the noise of the zipper as she was sealed up in the body bag.

"She was just a baby," she said, fighting the urge to roll down the window and scream it aloud. "Just four years old." She slapped her hand against the dash, hard enough for it to hurt. "Jesus, but she didn't deserve this to happen."

"No one does."

"I know," she breathed the words, leaning back in the seat, hands in her lap.

"You figure he's done it before?"

"Maybe," she said quietly, thinking of the missing boy in Pecan Creek, of all the other reports on missing or murdered children they'd culled from neighboring jurisdictions since

Carrie's abduction.

Had he done this before? Had he planned it this way? Or had something gone wrong? Had she fought him? Was that when he'd hit her with the brick?

"...If you ever tell your mommy, you'll lose her, too, you know...."

"Stop it," she whispered.

"You say something, Ryan?"

She hadn't realized she'd spoken aloud, and glanced at Phillips. "We have to stop him," she said, her heart pounding. "He has to be stopped before he does it again."

Chapter Ten

Maggie asked Phillips to take her over to the Spencers'.

"We have to look at the family, you know," he was saying as he drove. "Remember that case in South Carolina where the mother killed her own kids then lied to cover her own ass?"

"Ellen Spencer didn't do this," she told him, staring out the window, the passing houses and trees and street signs all a blur. "She loved her daughter."

"We should think about doing a polygraph."

"Jesus, John."

"Not all mothers are good mothers, Maggie."

"I know," she said quietly. "I know."

He turned off Woodlawn onto Sparrow and brought the car to a dead stop.

Maggie threw a hand up to the dash to brace herself, wondering what the hell he was doing. And then she saw it, too.

"Shit," he breathed.

It looked like rush-hour traffic on the Spencers' street.

Media vans had double-parked so that it was impossible for anything wider than a bicycle to pass through.

"Goddamned vultures must've picked up on their fucking scanners." He shook his head, adding another, "Shit," for good measure.

The sight made her stomach turn, and Maggie wanted to get out of there and quick.

"I'll meet you inside," she said, already opening the door, scrambling out of the Ford before Phillips could stop her.

She cut between a pair of cars and criss-crossed the lawn of the house two doors down. A dog barked at her from the other side of a board-on-board fence as she took a shortcut to the rear alley.

At least the reporters hadn't sunk to digging through anyone's trash yet, she thought as she walked past neat brick dumpsters filled with bagged garbage, wondering how they could live with themselves, how they could sleep at night, when they spent their days harassing victims all in the name of ratings. She could only imagine if one of their children had been killed, knowing then it would be a different story.

She tried to calm down as she walked, but there was too much inside her. Her heart hammered in her chest, and her mind reeled with thoughts of Carrie, of her lifeless face.

She rounded the six-foot high fence that caged in the Spencers' backyard. She found the gate, and, when the latch came open with a click, she let herself in.

The dry grass crunched beneath her feet as she bypassed the swingset heading toward a small concrete patio where a pair of whitewashed wrought iron chairs without cushions were pushed close to the house.

She went nearer the sliding glass doors and saw the flicker of the television screen in an otherwise dark den. Jake Spencer sprawled on the floor, propped up against the sofa.

Maggie rapped on the glass.

He didn't seem to hear her at first, so she tapped again, harder.

This time, he glanced over, his eyes wide.

She withdrew her ID from her purse and pressed her shield to the glass.

Slowly, Jake got up off the floor and walked over, flipping up the Charlie bar, unlocking the door, and sliding it open.

"You couldn't go to the front like everyone else?" he said, scowling at her as she came inside.

"I don't like crowds," she told him, not taking his bait. She locked the door again and bolted the Charlie bar in place.

Jake scooped up the remote control from the floor and dropped down on the couch, flinging a leg over its arm. "My mom's not here, you know. She and my dad are down at the morgue."

He said it without inflection, as if it were no different than them having gone up the block to the grocery store. Reds and yellows and blues and greens from the television flickered across his face, so that she couldn't read what was there, couldn't clearly see his eyes.

He hit the remote again, and music filled the room, thundering drums and guitars and screeching voices.

"Can I talk to you a minute?" she shouted above the din, but he acted as though she wasn't there.

There was a light switch near the door, and she flipped it on.

Jake blinked like a bat in sunlight.

Then she walked over to the TV set, found the power button, and pushed.

The screen went black. The noise died.

"What the hell're you doing?"

"I want to talk," she said. "About your sister." She crossed the room toward him, sidestepping throw pillows and motorcycle magazines.

"You got a warrant or something?"

Maggie stood above him, looking down. "I don't need a warrant just to ask a few questions."

"I already talked to you once. I told you I didn't know nothing."

"Well, I think you might." She pulled a plaid ottoman nearer to him and sat down. Dropping her purse at her feet, she rummaged for her pen and notebook.

Jake dragged himself into an upright position so that she got a good view of the skull and crossbones stretched across the chest of his black tee-shirt. He bent his knees and looped his arms around them. "I don't have to do this," he said, but he sounded less sure than his words. "You can't make me, you know. I'm just a kid. You can't push me around. That's harassment."

"You watch too much TV," she told him, thinking he was a prime example of the generation of couch potatoes, kids who'd grown up learning the lyrics of every television theme song, but not knowing how to read and write.

"What if I don't feel like talking?" he said. "What if I've got nothing to say?"

"Let's give it a try, okay?"

"Why don't you just leave me alone, pig?"

When Maggie didn't react to his provocation, he got up and started toward the door.

"We could always do this at the station," she said to his back. "Detective Phillips and I would be glad to take you with us. We'll keep you company till your folks can get there."

He stopped, standing still.

"Come on and sit down," she said, keeping her voice firm but even. "It won't take long. I promise."

He didn't move at first. The slim shoulders beneath his tee-shirt stiffened. His jeans were too long for him, slouching down around his ankles. His shoelaces dragged on the floor.

"Jake?"

He sighed and turned around, his cheeks flushed beneath the overgrown bangs.

With a grunt, he flung himself down on the sofa, slouching, arms across his chest.

Maggie ignored his obvious posturing, getting right to the point. "Did you see your sister at the park on Saturday?"

"I dunno. I could of, I guess." He started picking at a scab on his hand. "I was on my bike, man, so I just, you know, rode around. How many times have I gotta tell you guys this?"

"As many times as we ask."

He rolled his eyes, then stared up at the ceiling.

Maggie wondered how he could be so cool, so indifferent, when his parents were at the county morgue identifying his sister's remains. Carrie had been found dead this morning, and Jake was watching MTV like it was any other afternoon—any other day. Was that his defense mechanism? To repress? To pretend like he didn't give a damn?

Or maybe, she thought, he just didn't give a damn.

"Did you see Tyler Vincent at the park?"

"Tyler?" He wrinkled up his forehead. He glanced away from her and shrugged. "Maybe I did."

"What was he doing?"

"He was on his dirtbike, all right? Hauling ass around the neighborhood."

"Did you see anyone who seemed out of place?"

Jake laughed. "Except me, you mean?" His voice was clearly bitter.

Part of Maggie felt sorry for him. It didn't take much to realize he was unhappy, though she couldn't begin to guess why. There were probably a million reasons. There always were. Daddy didn't pay enough attention. Mommy didn't praise enough or punished too often. Or maybe he'd eaten too many lead-tainted crayons.

"Were you close to your sister?"

"Me and Carrie?" His smirky expression turned incredulous. "She was a midget, for God's sake. How was I supposed to get tight with a four-year-old brat?"

"Are you sorry she's dead."

He threw the pillow aside. "What d'you want me to say? That I'm glad?"

"Are you?" Maggie watched him. "I never had a sister, so I don't know how you must feel."

He ran his hands through his hair. "Everything in this fucking house centered on Carrie, you understand?" his voice was low, fingers kneading his neck. "She was a pain in the ass, you know?" He got up, clenching his fists, challenging her with his eyes. "So're you gonna arrest me for that?"

Maggie sighed, closing her notebook and sliding the pen up its spine. "No, Jake," she told him. "I'm not going to arrest you."

He seemed to relax.

She looked on him now and thought of when she'd first seen him in the kitchen. He'd been pretty dishevelled, his sneakers muddy, dirty jacket.

Her brain kicked into its "what if" mode, and she didn't like what she came up with.

He could have easily led his little sister away from the park. He could have put her on his bike with him. Only, maybe she got scared, maybe she started acting up and lost her shoe, her hair ribbon. He might not have thought of killing her, not at first, but if things went too far, if Carrie was frightened enough to cry out...

"Detective?"

His voice broke her thoughts, and she brushed her hair behind her ear.

"Can I go now?"

She'd seen boys younger than Jake shoot people cold and not shed a tear. And half the time, they killed for nothing. Just for the hell of it. For the thrill.

Maggie stared up at Jake, wondering if he had it in him.

"Did you take Carrie from the park?" she asked.

"You think I killed her?"

"Did you?"

His eyes narrowed and something flickered within them. She expected him to shout at her, to curse her, but he did neither.

Carrie's face flashed in her mind again, its bluish cast,

93

the purple welt on her forehead, the eyes wide open and staring, and she tasted bile in her throat.

She pushed down the nausea, her voice sounding hoarse as she asked again, "Did you take your sister from the park?"

"Fuck off," Jake said and left.

Maggie found Phillips sitting in the living room with Barbara Vincent.

"Detective Ryan?" She looked confused, her forehead creasing as Maggie settled down beside her partner on the Queen Anne-style sofa. "When'd you get here?"

"Jake let me in," she explained, saying nothing about the conversation she'd had with him.

Barbara shook her head. "God, but I can't even keep track of everyone comin' and goin'. Between the neighbors and the police, and now those damned reporters." She pursed her lips, the cords in her neck tensing. "It's awful, isn't it? This whole thing's a nightmare."

Mrs. Vincent appeared as if she'd been kept awake by the very nightmare she talked about. There were gray half-moons beneath her eyes, and her skin looked pale and pinched.

"I just can't believe this has all happened right here in Litchfield," she went on, her drawl softer, less strident than it had been when Maggie had met her on Saturday evening. "Makes me scared to death, seein' as how my Ashley is the same age as Carrie is." She glanced down. "I mean, was."

She fingered the flame-stitched fabric on the arms of the wing chair, going on as if talking to herself. "They probably wish they'd never moved here from Greenwich. Ellen didn't want to leave anyway. Said she got hysterical when Tom told her they were comin' to Dallas." She fiddled with a gold bracelet that curled around her wrist like a snake. "Ellen lived there her whole life. Her parents still own the same house she grew up in." She lifted her head, and her sad eyes met Maggie's. "Tom's position, that's the explanation she gave me. He had to start over again. Though she never said why."

"Do you mind if I ask you some questions, Mrs. Vincent?" Maggie said, trying not to push, but needing something more than she had.

Barbara cocked her head, looking puzzled at first, then affronted. "I don't know as that's real appropriate, Detective, what with Carrie...with her bein' found just this morning, and Ellen down at the morgue with Tom. Dear Lord..." she looked at Phillips for support.

Phillips cleared his throat. "I'm a father myself, Mrs. Vincent. Got two girls of my own. I want whoever did this caught as fast as anybody. And if we're going to do that, we need to get as much information as we can from the people who knew Carrie best."

"I told all I know already," she protested, but there was no fight in her voice. She shifted in her seat, pulling at her sweater. "I guess it couldn't hurt for you to ask again."

"Thank you," Maggie said, and nodding appreciatively at Phillips.

Her notebook on her lap, she flipped through it, finding a clean sheet of paper. "You said you were talking with Ellen Spencer while Carrie was playing?"

"Ashley was there too," Barb interrupted, her sharp features screwing up in concentration. "Scramblin' around like a monkey on the jungle gym."

"And you didn't see anything or anyone suspicious?"

Barb put a manicured nail to her chin, tapping thoughtfully. "I don't recall anything out of the ordinary, same as I told you before. Everyone I saw either belonged there or looked like they did."

Maggie looked up. "Which means what exactly?"

"You know perfectly well what I'm talkin' about, Detective," she said, her expression sober. "If I'd of seen anyone dressed funny, walking funny, driving a funny car, I wouldn't forget it. We're as close-knit a neighborhood as they come these days. We keep an eye out for each other."

But not close enough, Maggie thought. No one had watched Carrie Spencer being led away. She was beginning to think the whole neighborhood lived by the credo of, "hear no evil, see no evil, think no evil." Between her and Phillips, they'd interviewed the entire subdivision, and neither of them had hit upon a single soul who could offer anything but sympathy.

"How old is your son?" she asked.

Barb rubbed her palms over her knees. "Tyler's fifteen. He's been helping out with the flyers. Didn't you already speak with him, Detective?"

Maggie remembered a slim boy with brown hair and bluejeans. "Was he at the park on Saturday?"

Barb chewed on her lip. "Didn't I mention that before? I can't recall if I did or not. He was ridin' around on that dirtbike his daddy gave him last Christmas. He's always out doin' something, if he's not squirreled up in his room with that computer of his."

"So he was at the park?"

"He might've driven by, but I can't recall getting more than a glimpse of him. I'm sure the last thing he was thinkin' of doing was coming round to where us mothers sit and joining us." She smiled, slightly. "You know how boys are at his age," she said, looking over at Phillips, as if he surely must remember.

"Would you mind if I talked to him again?" Maggie asked.

"He's across the street watching Ashley. Frank drove Ellen and Tom to the...to make a positive identification." Barb sighed loudly, turning her head toward the window. She was quiet for a few minutes, and Maggie caught Phillips checking his Timex.

Barbara brushed at her cheeks. "Tyler babysat for Ellen, maybe once or twice a month. They didn't trust Jake to stay alone with his sister." She hesitated, as if deciding whether or not to confide something to them, apparently deeming them trustworthy enough to confess in a whisper, "I don't know how Ellen puts up with him. He's out of control. The way he talks to her...the things he says." She clasped her hands in her lap.

"Has he been in trouble?"

"Trouble?" Her eyes widened, and Maggie thought she looked frightened. "Jake's not...well, he isn't a nice kid. He picks fights. Skips school. He was just hateful to Carrie. I think that's why Ellen was afraid to leave him alone with the child." She drew in a breath, then let it out slowly. "Someone killed some cats and dogs around the neighborhood awhile back. No one said as much aloud, but everyone figured it was Jake. At least I did."

Phillips nudged Maggie. "Happened about five or six months ago, didn't it?"

"Sounds about right."

It had made the local paper, even the *Dallas Morning News* had picked it up. Maggie recalled that Leonard and Washington had done a cursory investigation, but nothing came of it.

"I appreciate your help, Mrs. Vincent," Maggie told her, closing up her notebook and returning it to her purse.

Barb stood up, brushing at the creases in her slacks. "Now, if you'll excuse me, I've got things to do. Ellen's folks are flying in later on, and there's the service..." her voice caught, and she hurried from the room without another word.

"I'll be right back," Maggie said to Phillips, picking up her purse as she rose from the couch.

"Hey, where're you going now?"

"Across the street to talk to Tyler."

"Detective Ryan!" someone cried out as Maggie emerged from the house. Before she'd even stepped off the front stoop, the press converged on her.

Cameras swung in her direction. Microphones jabbed in her face, bumping her nose.

"Jesus Christ," she said, waving her hands in front of her. "Back off."

"Was Carrie Spencer raped, Detective?" one woman shouted.

"Can you tell us how was she killed?" another yelled.

Maggie fought her way through them, saying, "No comment," again and again like a mantra, until they gave up on her, and she broke free, hiking her bag up on her shoulder as she headed across the street.

When she reached the curb, she paused to catch her breath. She looked up at the Vincent house, taking it in. Red brick with two stories, it was a mirror image of the Spencers', what people around here sometimes called a "Dallas Palace." A mix—or rather mangling—of architectural styles that had evolved into a style all its own.

The flat heels of her loafers clicked noisily on the cobblestone driveway as she approached the front door. A silver-gray Jaguar blocked her way, and she stopped to check it out, peering through the smoky windows at what looked like burgundy leather. She whistled softly. Barb's car, she guessed, since Mr. Vincent had apparently driven the Spencers down to the morgue. She ran a finger along the body as she rounded the hood. If this was one of the perks of being a housewife in the suburbs, no wonder there was a backlash against feminism these days.

Huge pots filled with newly-planted pansies flanked the entranceway, and Maggie figured a gardener had done the digging, not Mrs. Vincent with her painted fingernails.

She rang the bell and waited, until the door came open as wide as a chain would allow it. A hazel eye gave her the once-over. "You a reporter?"

Maggie smiled. "I could take that as an insult, you know," she said, digging into her purse and drawing out her badge and ID. She held them up so they could be seen. "I'm Detective Ryan from the Litchfield PD."

"Oh, yeah." The voice sounded contrite. "Sorry, about that. My mom just called and said you'd be over. Hold on, okay?" he said and closed the door in her face.

It opened again, minus the chain. Tyler Vincent stood there in his bare feet. He wore a Dallas Cowboys sweatshirt and jeans that bunched around his ankles, like Jake's. He shrugged, looking uncomfortable. "Come in, I guess," he said.

She walked past him into the foyer. Each footstep seemed to echo on the marble tiles. No wonder Tyler was barefoot. Although the layout was much like the Spencers, the decor of this house was over the top. A grand staircase curved upward to the second floor. Foil-flocked paper covered walls that soared upward to at least fifteen feet. Overhead, a chandelier dripped tiers of crystals, the light so bright that, when Maggie turned away, she saw stars.

"The family room, okay?" he asked

Maggie nodded. "Fine."

"This way." She followed him, past an ornate dining room and through a hallway filled with expensively framed photographs.

They entered into a cavernous room with mauve-colored walls and plush furniture in Navajo patterns. A big screen TV and elaborate stereo system filled custom-built shelves.

She took a seat on the nearer of two sofas. "Where's Ashley?" she asked as Tyler perched on a chair set catty-corner.

"She's in her room," he said, "Upstairs. Taking a nap."

Maggie retrieved her notebook, thinking that would at least make things easier.

"You want something to drink?"

"No, thanks."

He nodded, wiping his hands on his thighs. "It sucks," he said, and Maggie met his eyes. "About Carrie."

"You used to sit with her, didn't you?"

"Mrs. Spencer didn't like to leave her alone with Jake." He shrugged. "I didn't mind. She was a good kid, you know?"

There was real pain in his face, and Maggie got the impression at once that this fifteen-year-old kid had cared more for Carrie than her own brother.

"How was Jake with her, exactly?"

He frowned, but didn't look up. "He called her names, yelled at her sometimes."

"Did he ever hurt her?"

"Hurt her?" Tyler hesitated, then shook his head. "Jake tries to be a hard-ass, you know? But he's not as bad as everyone thinks."

Not as bad? In comparison to whom? she wondered. Charlie Manson?

"You were riding your dirtbike on Saturday, right?"

He raised his eyes to hers. "I've been trying to think hard, like everyone's asked me to. But I don't remember seeing anything weird that afternoon. I don't even think I saw Carrie."

"Did you see Jake?"

"At the park, you mean?"

Maggie nodded.

"He was on his bike, right? Yeah, we might've passed on the street a time or two. But we weren't hanging together or anything."

The silver-framed photographs that filled the coffee table caught Maggie's eye, and she leaned over, picking up the nearest one.

The picture was black and white, of a little girl, shot upward from her feet, so the clouds seemed to hang right above her head, the sun hidden, but the light of its rays creating a sort of halo around her.

"Is this Ashley?" she asked.

"Uh-huh."

"She's a cute kid."

He half-smiled. "She's not bad for a sister."

Maggie set it aside and picked up another, recognizing Barbara and Frank Vincent in formal attire, looking very much like a mature Barbie and Ken. The effect almost surreal.

Picture perfect, she mused as she put it back in its place, thinking that the same could be said of the Spencers and probably every other family on the block. Only she knew it was less truth than image.

She turned back to Tyler.

"You certain you didn't see anything that stuck out as odd while you were near the park on Saturday?"

"No, nothing."

"If you do think of something, even if it doesn't seem like much to you, please give me a call at the station, all right?"

"Sure thing," he said and stood up, hooking his thumbs in the waistband of his jeans.

Maggie put away her notebook and lifted her purse, retracing the path they'd taken earlier, Tyler right on her heels.

She walked into the foyer and looked up.

A little girl stood on the steps, holding onto the curving banister. Her face was round, her eyes wide. Brown hair hung in tangles to her shoulders. Her cheeks were pink and tear-stained.

Maggie stared.

The child wore only a tee-shirt and pink underpants.

Her pudgy legs were bare.

"Ash? What're you doing down here?" Tyler came around from behind Maggie's back. "Go upstairs," he said, heading toward the steps.

"I want Mommy. I want Mommy." the small voice rose to a near wail.

"Ash, please," Tyler tried again and started after her.

She saw him coming and let go of the bannister, scurrying on up the stairs.

With a loud sigh, Tyler turned around, his hands shoved in his pockets. "She has nightmares now," he told her, "even in the daytime."

Maggie's heart ached. "I can't blame her," she whispered. "I have nightmares about Carrie, too."

Chapter Eleven

Maggie stared out the window as Phillips drove to the station. This wasn't right. This whole thing wasn't right. Someone had stolen a little girl from a public park, had taken her five miles away to a construction site and had killed her, all without leaving a clue.

She leaned her brow against the cool glass, wondering if Carrie had been afraid of the dark, frightened to go to sleep at night, too.

"Ryan? You want to talk about it?"

"Talk about what?" She raised her head, rubbing at the ache behind her eyes.

He steered with one hand, gesturing aimlessly with the other one. "What's eating at you."

"I'm fine."

He pulled up at a stop sign, taking his eyes off the road long enough to look at her. "At least tell me what happened with the boy."

"With Tyler?"

"No," he said, "Jake."

Maggie sighed, squinting at the glare of sunlight on the windshield, wondering how to explain to him what she'd gotten out of Jake, when what she felt was just that: feelings, not facts. She settled for, "I think he's a real mixed up kid."

"Mixed up enough to kill his little sister?"

"I don't know," she said, squirming against the confining seatbelt, trying to figure out if Jake was really capable of such a thing, or if his attitude of I-don't-give-a-damn was simply an act he put on to keep people at a distance.

He was jealous of Carrie. That much, he'd admitted. What had he called her? A midget. A pain in the ass. Not exactly loving descriptions.

Nor were Barbara Vincent's remarks about him. She'd made Jake sound like the neighborhood terror, picking fights, causing trouble.

Maggie would have to pull the file on the animal killings, read over the reports. What if Jake *were* responsible, as Barb Vincent had suggested? Would that prove he was capable of murdering a child?

"He's angry," she said aloud.

Phillips laughed. "Isn't that a requirement for teenagers today? God, but I hate to think of my girls growing up now. All the pressures." He exhaled. "It's almost scary to be a child."

Scary to be a child. She rubbed at her eyes. Christ, she was so tired. What's wrong with you, Maggie? she asked herself. Getting burned out at the ripe old age of twenty-nine?

The blinker clicked as Phillips turned the corner, bumping over the uneven pavement into the parking lot. He pulled past a pair of blue-and-whites, settling into a space behind them. Then he shut the engine off and got out.

The Ford shuddered as he slammed the door.

Her own door squeaked open, and Phillips held it wide for her, leaning in. "You coming, Ryan?"

Maggie shook off her thoughts, grabbed her bag and climbed out. She hurried ahead of him into the building, avoiding the crowd that converged on the front desk, most of them reporters.

Greg Leonard intercepted them as they came through the security door. "Some of the blood work's back. Captain's already been briefed. Sarge wants to see you in his office."

Phillips pushed Maggie forward as they followed Leonard to the sergeant's office. He sat behind a paper-cluttered desk, glancing up as they entered. Several chairs had been drawn up around him. Harold Washington occupied one of them, his notebook open on his knees, his dark features somber. Leonard sauntered over and took a seat next to Washington, crossing his arms.

Maggie and Phillips settled down beside him.

"They've analyzed the shoe?" she asked, pulling out her notebook, so anxious for some good news her chest tightened.

"Just preliminary stuff," Leonard clarified. "First of all, the stain on the sneaker was blood. It's been sent down to Harris County for DNA testing. Their equipment's better than anything we have access to up here. Could take a few weeks at least."

Weeks? That was time they didn't have.

"And the ribbon?" she asked.

Sarge picked up a folder, shuffling through the enclosed pages. "The hairs match the victim's, which is what we expected. There were some carpet fibers on the shoe, so we're checking them against the wall-to-wall at the Spencers'."

"Any prints on the rubber sole?"

"None that we can use," he told her, matter-of-fact, his bulldog-face unsmiling. "Kids walk through puddles, play in the mud. There wasn't even a readable partial."

Maggie grasped for something more, anything. "What about clothing fibers? Hairs that weren't Carrie's?"

Sarge shook his head. "Nothing that gets us anywhere. And the trace evidence from the scene is about worthless, what with all the debris from the construction site and the people tracking through it."

"You said the stain on her shoe was blood," she pressed on, unwilling to give up. "Did they type it?"

"It's O positive, which happens to match with the victim."

"Not to mention half the population," Phillips remarked under his breath. Maggie's mouth went dry.

"Like Leonard said, the DNA lab in Harris County is running tests, but we won't get results for awhile. Could be weeks," Sarge reminded them, and Maggie nodded.

"So we don't know if the blood is hers or her killer's?"

Greg Leonard crossed his arms over his wrinkled button-down shirt and loosened tie. "Ryan, you're a genius."

Her cheeks warmed, but she didn't let him bait her. She was too unsettled by the lack of evidence. They had nothing to go on. No starting point.

Phillips spoke up in a weary voice that mirrored

Maggie's own frustration. "Any good news?"

"Maybe there is." Harold Washington flipped through his notes. "The fibbies turned up something on one of the soccer coaches who was at Litchfield Park on Saturday afternoon with a team from the local Y." He pulled some folded papers from his notebook, passing several to Maggie. She gave one to Phillips, then looked down at her own. "His name's Brian Westmoreland. Twenty-five years old. He got early parole a month ago."

Maggie stared at the page in her hands. "Jesus." She studied the black and white mug shots of a frowning young man, then ran a finger down the computerized rap sheet. "How could something like this have happened?"

Leonard laughed. "Hell, Ryan, he only served a third-time because he was such a good boy."

"He raped children," she said aloud, still not believing what she saw with her own eyes. "He's got priors, goddammit...three counts of indecency with a child."

Sarge's high-backed chair squeaked as he clasped his hands behind his head. "We all know it happens everyday. Deals get cut. Prisons fill up, and they need the space." He shrugged. "Hell, child molestation's not even a federal crime. No one wants to believe pedophiles are all bad. They're bankers and lawyers, right?"

Phillips whispered, "And priests."

She shook her head.

It wasn't right. None of it made sense.

No child deserved to end up like Carrie had. No child invited abuse, despite the excuses she'd heard molesters give time and again.

"She spread her legs when I changed her diapers...he kept playing with himself when I gave him a bath...you'd understand if you'd seen the way she wiggled in my lap."

"You know it's only because I love you...."

No, she thought. It wasn't love.

It was sick.

Sarge dispatched a patrol car to pick up Brian Westmoreland, and Maggie waited at her desk, trying to get some work done in the meantime, but she was too edgy.

Phillips brought a cup of coffee over. "Drink up," he said. "You look like you could use it."

Instead, Maggie warmed her hands on the styrofoam cup. "How could they do it, John? Hiring someone to work with kids without doing a background check?"

Phillips sat down on the edge of her desk. "People are lazy, Maggie."

"So it takes time..."

"And time is money."

She pushed away the coffee and put her head in her hands, catching her fingers in her shaggy brown curls. "I just don't understand."

"Politics, Ryan," he whispered. "That's what it all boils down to. Until the powers-that-be tell the ACLU to fuck off and get their priorities straight, the criminals have all the rights."

She propped her chin on her fists. "You know what, Phillips?"

"What?"

"Life sucks."

He laughed. "Is that supposed to be news?"

She pushed her hair out of her eyes, opening up her notebook, full of her scribbles from the past several days.

Phillips pulled up a chair, and they went over what they had so far, from their first visit with the Spencers the night Carrie was reported missing to this morning's discovery of her body and their subsequent conversations with Barbara Vincent, Tyler, and Jake.

They were still talking it over when Greg Leonard approached, snapping his fingers to get their attention.

"He's here," he said, and Maggie was instantly out of her chair, leaving her notebook lying open on her desk. Phillips was on his feet just as fast.

"He was at the Y teaching a gym class for some day care kids. Would you fucking believe it?" Leonard went on as they headed toward the interview room. "He came along real easy, they said. He didn't want to make a scene," he spat out the last word, the disgust in his voice all too evident. He paused outside the door with his hand on the knob. "Oh, and Sarge wants you in there, Ryan. You and Phillips. He thinks Westmoreland might open up more if there's a woman around."

He pushed wide the door to the interview room, and swept a meaty hand before him, the ever-present smirk on his face, as if everything were a joke and Maggie was the punchline.

A camera would tape Westmoreland's every move—and her own. And she knew there'd be a crowd watching through the one-way glass, so she steeled herself, straightening her back and lifting her chin, forcing a facade of confidence even if she didn't quite feel it.

"I'm right behind you," Phillips said in her ear, his breath stirring her hair.

She stepped into the room no bigger than her own walk-in closet. The walls were covered in a carpet-like fabric to stifle sound.

Brian Westmoreland turned his head, shifting his gaze in her direction. He sat in one of the chairs beside a small table. In front of him was a styrofoam cup filled with water.

Maggie thought of the copies of his rap sheet she'd seen not a half-hour before and wondered how on earth someone who looked so benign could be so lethal.

Like most, he seemed different in person, less evil than the man in the mug shot. His hair was trimmed short, his jaw close-shaven. But the frown was the same, as were the close-set eyes that watched her as she settled into the chair across from his, their knees practically touching.

His skin was lightly freckled, and in some ways he didn't even appear the twenty-five years she knew him to be. It was no wonder children trusted him. He could be their big brother.

"No one's read me m' rights," he said, his drawl thick and lazy, hardly menacing in any way. Still, Maggie prickled at the sound of his voice.

"You're not under arrest, Brian," she said, taking the lead. Phillips sat down beside her and leaned toward the suspect. "We just wanted to talk to you. We thought you might be able to help us. You can leave any time you want."

The suspect's expression was uneasy. "This about the

missin' kid?"

"Yes. Did you know her?"

"Did I know her?"

"Carrie Spencer."

"The little girl?" He cocked his head. "Hell, everyone in town knows who she is. Her picture's been plastered in the papers and on the TV for two solid days."

Maggie fought to keep her voice steady, and her face as stoic as possible. She could smell his sweat. He breathed through his mouth, making raspy little noises.

"Did you know Carrie?" she asked. "Maybe she'd been to the Y?"

"I've only worked here a couple weeks. I was stayin' with my sister before that. I hardly know everyone in Litchfield." He shrugged. "I might've seen her around, I guess."

Maggie watched his eyes, how they shifted from her to Phillips and back again. "You were at Litchfield Park on Saturday. The day she was abducted." It was a statement not a question, and Westmoreland looked suddenly agitated at the obvious connection.

He wrapped his fingers around the cup of water. "I was coaching a soccer game. We'd been playing indoors, but the weather was nice so we moved the games outside."

"Did you see Carrie Spencer at the park that day, Brian?"

A nervous smile crossed his lips. "I'm supposed to remember seeing one little girl, when there were dozens of kids running around?"

Maggie's insides felt twisted, her head pounded. He

was a practiced liar, she was sure. All pedophiles were. They had to be to get away with what they did, luring little boys and girls into their web and then frightening them so that they were afraid to speak out. "You like children, don't you?"

His eyes went to Phillips again, as if he might find safety there. He kept wiping his palms on his sweatpants. "Yeah, I like children. I'm good with kids."

Phillips passed over a piece of paper, and Maggie held it out to Westmoreland. "Well, I think maybe you like kids a little too much."

"What's that supposed to mean?" His protest died as he took the page from her hand. His eyes skimmed up and down it, before he stared across the wrinkled sheet at Maggie, his face a vivid pink. He looked for a moment as if he would explode, and Maggie braced herself, ready for it. Then, as quickly, the fire went out of his eyes and he set the paper aside on the table as casually as if it were a magazine.

"You haven't got anything on me," he said, his voice rising at the end, so that she wasn't sure if he was asking or telling. "This is harassment, that's what it is. And if you keep it up, I'll lose my job." He pushed a hand through his hair, clearly ruffled. "I turned my life around, you hear me? I did everything they asked."

Maggie fought to keep still.

"What went on in the past...it doesn't prove I had anything to do with what happened to that girl...whoever she is."

"Carrie," she reminded him. "Carrie Spencer."

"You can't pin it on me."

Maggie leaned nearer him. "I will if you did it."

He crossed his arms over his chest, his face hardening.

"I don't have to answer any more of your questions. Not without a lawyer."

"I already told you once, Brian, you're not under arrest."

"It sure feels like it."

Maggie pushed her chair back and stood, looking down at him. But Westmoreland kept his eyes on the floor.

"I have a feeling I'll be seeing you again."

"C'mon," Phillips said to her. "It stinks in here."

She pressed open the door, stepping into the hallway, her chest so tight she could hardly breathe.

"You went easy on him, Ryan."

Leonard was waiting for her in the hallway.

"Shouldn't let a woman do a man's job, right, John?" he said and started laughing.

Maggie's skin burned.

Phillips came up beside her, and she felt the tips of his fingers at her back.

"Excuse me," she said, ignoring both of them.

She hurried up the hallway, escaping into the restroom. She turned on the tap, gripping either side of the small porcelain sink as water gushed from the spigot. She splashed her face over and over, but still she felt hot. She was furious. She shut off the water and leaned forward, touching her forehead to the mirrored-glass, closing her eyes.

"You're so pretty, little Magpie. I can't help what I do, don't you see?"

"Detective Ryan?"

Maggie jerked, looking up and into the mirror to find another face reflected near her own.

114

"Are you all right?"

Maggie let out a breath and turned around, her lower back against the sink. "Jesus, Susie, you scared me."

The dispatcher shrugged, grinning apologetically. "Sorry, Maggie," she said and then disappeared into one of the stalls.

Maggie pulled some brown paper towels from the dispenser, wiping off her face, drying her hands, thinking about what Brian Westmoreland had told her, knowing it was more than he realized. Hoping it was enough.

Chapter Twelve

Maggie was going over the transcript of her interview with Westmoreland, when her phone buzzed.

She punched the line and picked up. "Maggie Ryan," she said.

"Margaret?"

She put the pages down, the familiar sinking feeling sliding into her gut. "Momma..."

"It's gone again," she started off, rushing on as if she could hardly catch her breath. "They took my gold watch, Margaret. I put it on my dresser last night, and this morning it was gone."

"Momma, I can't talk now." Maggie turned around in her chair, away from the rest of the room, keeping her voice low. "I'm at work..."

"They were in the house!"

"No one was there, Momma. Try looking in the sugar bowl, that's where it was the last time."

She was crying now. "I'm frightened, Margaret."

"Momma, please, let me talk to Delores..."

The line clicked off.

Maggie rolled the receiver away from her ear. This was a bad dream, right? Just part of the nightmares she'd been having.

Her other line lit up, blinking red, and she sighed, reaching over to push the button.

"Ryan," she said, trying to shake off her mother's call and settle back into her skin.

She heard heavy breathing and knew someone was there, but no one spoke. She sat up straighter, feeling her heart pound. "Detective Ryan, Litchfield Police," she said for good measure. Jesus, she didn't have time for this.

"How the hell could it have happened?" The words were a low moan. "Why would anyone want to hurt her?"

Maggie struggled to recognize the voice: ragged, raspy as a lifelong smoker. "I didn't get your name..." she tried the easiest route.

"Why're you just sitting around when there's a killer out there somewhere?" he lashed out. "Why aren't you doing something to find him?"

And then she knew who it was. Carrie's father.

Shit.

"She was just four-years-old, goddammit," he said, his voice breaking. He began sobbing, and she felt suddenly guilty, as if she were somehow to blame for the death of his little girl. As if she had failed.

"I'm sorry," she said softly, wishing it could have turned out differently, taking it more personally than she should. "I'm so sorry about Carrie. We're doing everything we can..."

"Are you?"

"Yes." She wrinkled up her brow, not liking where this was heading.

"It's easy for you to say that, isn't it? It's not your daughter who's there in the morgue," he whispered hoarsely. "It's not your life that's torn apart."

She wrapped the telephone cord around her finger, twisting it till her skin turned blue, and then unwinding it again. She wanted to say something to comfort him, to reassure him, but she couldn't find the words.

"Oh, God," he moaned, his voice slurred so that she wondered if he'd taken something for his pain and only made it worse. "I should've been there, then maybe it would have been different. Maybe Carrie'd be safe now."

Maggie sensed something. "You were at Methodist, weren't you?"

"Yes."

"You were there all day?"

"Yes."

"But you never phoned your wife that afternoon when Carrie disappeared, though she said she'd paged you for nearly an hour. Were you in surgery, perhaps..."

"I'm not a surgeon," he murmured, sounding confused. "I'm an internist."

"Do you work with children?"

"No...sometimes."

"So you were on the hospital campus all day?"

"I don't...I didn't..." he stopped, seeming to catch himself. Trying to sober up? "I went to my office...it's across the street...I did some paperwork."

"Did anyone see you there?" she asked.

"I don't know..."

"You showed up at home without ever having returned your wife's page. Maybe you were in the area?"

She could hear his noisy breaths, but he didn't answer. Maggie knew she was pushing it, using his weakness, but she couldn't stop. "Did you know your wife had taken Carrie to the park?"

"Why are you doing this?" There was such pain in his voice that Maggie felt she'd gone too far. "For God's sake, she was my daughter."

"I'm sorry..."

"Like hell you are," he cried, and the phone went dead. He'd hung up.

She slipped the receiver back onto its cradle.

Good going, Maggie.

She rubbed at the back of her neck, feeling a knot of tension as big as a gumball. Something bothered her about the call, about Tom Spencer. She'd had devastated parents bawl her out before, for not doing enough. It wasn't that. It was less what he said, than what he hadn't.

"...We should think about doing a polygraph..."

John Phillips' words returned to nag at her.

"...Not all mothers are good mothers..."

And all fathers weren't good fathers.

She glanced up and caught Phillips pointing to the phone he held to his ear.

Thank God for Ma Bell and her babies, she thought as she pushed back her chair. It seemed like they spent half their lives on the telephone.

She got up and went toward him, rounding a desk with a half-finished report rolled into an old IBM Selectric and a lipstick-stained mug of coffee on a paper-strewn blotter.

She came up behind his chair and peered over his shoulder, squinting at the notes he took as he talked, trying to decipher his illegible scribbles. But she gave up and sat down on the edge of his desk, waiting for him to finish up his call.

Her gaze wandered around the room.

The squad room was still in constant motion. Fax machines chattered. Computer keys clicked. Everyone was working overtime on double shifts, eager to nail whoever it was that had abducted and killed Carrie Spencer.

No one liked the idea of the girl's murderer being out there, free to cruise the streets of Litchfield or its neighboring cities, looking for his next victim.

Phillips slapped the phone down with a clatter, and Maggie turned to find him grinning like the Cheshire cat.

"You were right," he said and scratched his jaw, which had begun to sport a five o'clock shadow. "God, but you were right on the nose."

"I was?" She leaned toward him. "About what?"

"Westmoreland," he said, squirming in his seat as if he could hardly keep still. His eyes glinted, and he looked like a little boy on Christmas.

"Oh, God, you don't mean he confessed?" she blurted out, not waiting for him to finish.

"Whoa, slow down," he cut her off. "First things first." He settled back in his chair, tapping a pen against his notebook. "I spoke with a lady named Fairdale over at the Y where

Westmoreland works. She said he was supposed to bring back the soccer equipment right after the game, but he didn't show for over an hour. He told her he'd met some of the kids and their folks at a burger joint and lost track of time." He raised his eyebrows, and the leathery planes of his cheeks twitched. "Makes you wonder, doesn't it?"

He looked like he didn't believe Westmoreland's story, and Maggie wasn't sure she did either. "I'll have Ramsey check..."

He stopped her with a wave of his hand. He wasn't done. "There's more."

"Go on," she said. Her spine tingled.

"I called the parole board in Austin."

"And?"

"He's got a sister who lives in Pecan Creek."

Maggie stared at him.

"He stayed with her for awhile after he was cut loose. Remember how he'd said he only moved to Litchfield a couple weeks ago?"

"So he was in Pecan Creek when Kenny Wayne disappeared."

"Bingo."

"And he was at the park on Saturday when Carrie was snatched."

Phillips clasped his hands behind his head. "I'd say that's one hell of a coincidence, wouldn't you?"

"Jesus." Her mind spun. It was all happening so fast.

She reached for his phone, but he caught her hand before she'd even lifted the receiver. "What're you doing?"

"I want to call Pecan Creek, tell the sheriff what we

know."

"Hell, Ryan, it's taken care of already." He patted her hand, before she withdrew it. "I just got off the phone with Moody. I promised to fax a copy of Westmoreland's rap sheet. They're gonna' pass around his picture, see if anyone remembers him being in the area on the day Kenny Wayne up and vanished. I gave him a description of the car, too." He picked up his pen and rolled it in his palm. "They're gonna have a little chat with his sister. Try to shake her up a bit."

"What if he tries to skip?"

"We'll put a tail on him. If he makes a move, we'll be on him like flies on dogshit." He tipped his head, looking at her a little too closely, frowning. "Hey, Maggie, you don't look so hot. I'll bet you haven't eaten since breakfast."

He got up, yanking at his belt, though the soft overhang of his belly prevented it from moving up an inch. Then he nudged her gently.

"How 'bout if I buy you a sandwich? Vending machine's got tuna. Though it doesn't taste the same since they threw out the dolphins, does it?"

"Jesus, John."

"Well, it's the truth, isn't it?"

The sky was a murky black, starless from all the clouds that had swept in, covering up any trace of the moon in their wake. Maggie drove her Mazda through the pitch, its headlamps slicing through the ever-growing fogginess. She hadn't passed another car on the road. She was alone with her thoughts, and she had plenty of them to keep her company.

Brian Westmoreland's face filled her mind, and she wondered if it was the last thing Carrie had seen before she died. Had she trusted him enough to let him lead her from the park? With his soft drawl and freckled cheeks, would he have seemed safe to her? Had Kenny Wayne made the same mistake?

Maggie gripped the steering wheel tighter, thinking of his rap sheet, of the three counts of indecency with a child. No doubt there were others out there, more victims who'd kept quiet. That was an abuser's MO after all, to instill fear, to make children afraid.

And it worked.

The wind tugged at her coat as she left her car in the parking lot of her complex. She ducked her chin into her collar as she hurried up to her front door.

She slipped off her coat as soon as she'd locked herself in, and removed her .38 from her purse, unsnapping it from its holster, and taking it into her bedroom. She set it down on the nightstand.

The light on her answering machine flashed on and off, and she played back the messages, finding more than a few from reporters, several from Momma, and as many from Delores telling her to ignore everything her mother'd told her. The last was from Terry urging her to call no matter the time.

Maggie sat down on the bed, drawing her knees to her chest, and picked up the phone to dial Terry's number.

It rang but once before she heard her friend's gravelled, "Hello?"

"It's me," she said.

"Maggie?"

"Did I wake you?"

There was a muffled noise, another voice, then Terry said, "It's okay, really. I've got clients who call at all hours." She laughed quietly. "Dave just rolls over and goes back to sleep." She paused. "Hey, are you all right? I saw you on the news. You're pretty good with those 'no comments.'"

"They never get my best side."

Terry's voice turned tight. "I can't believe what's going on. It's terrifying."

It was more than that.

Maggie set her forehead on her knees and whispered, "I need your help."

"I'll be right over..."

"It's not about me," Maggie told her. "It's about the little girl who died. Carrie Spencer."

"What can I do?" she asked, so softly Maggie could barely hear her.

"I think he knew her. That she knew him. He got her away from the park without making a scene." Maggie stopped, hearing the rise and fall of her own voice, the noise of her heart, and forced herself to calm down. "Give me a profile of him, Terry."

"You probably know as much as I do."

"Please," she urged her. "It's important."

Terry sighed. "I used to think there was a single profile for pedophiles. But I'm not so sure any more. I mean, there's the standard line about sociopaths all being loners, but that doesn't say much of anything, does it?" She hesitated. "I worked with a boy who was eight when he started forcing sex on his baby sister. It took four years before anyone caught on. And this was a nice family, Mag—what we'd consider upper-middle class. Real upstanding." She stopped as if to get her thoughts in order, and then she said, "I know the answer you're looking for, and I can't give you that."

Maggie wouldn't give up. "Try."

"Okay, okay," Terry murmured, clearly reluctant. "This is straight from the textbooks, all right? He's probably a white male, maybe in his 20s or early 30s. He was most likely abused as a child, but that's not always the case. He's sexually confused, sexually repressed." She paused. "It's not something you can see in his face. It's inside him, whatever makes him tick."

Maggie interrupted. "He'd want to be close to children, wouldn't he? Maybe even get a job that puts him in daily contact with kids, so his behavior wouldn't be as suspect?"

"Yes."

Maggie thought of Brian Westmoreland working at the local Y, spending his days unsupervised with boys and girls whose parents trusted him. "If he killed Carrie Spencer, there's a chance he's done it before, right?"

"Well, it's possible, I guess."

"That's what I wanted to know, Terry. Thanks."

"Hey, Maggie, wait. I'm worried about you."

"I'm fine."

"Are you?"

"I swear."

Her voice was soft. "You lie."

Maggie told her goodbye and put the phone aside.

She stripped down to her cotton underpants and pulled on her flannel pajamas. Barefoot, she padded into the kitchen and heated up a bowl of soup, carrying it into the living room.

She turned on the TV just in time to catch the tail-end

of the late news, wincing at the sight of a windblown reporter standing in front of the Spencers' house; shutting the set off when they switched to a shot of a crying Ellen and stone-faced Tom Spencer emerging from the county morgue.

Setting her barely-touched soup on the coffee table, she slumped back against the sofa cushions and rubbed her hands over her face.

She knew the press would be out in full force at Carrie's funeral. They'd turn a private event into a three-ring circus.

She wondered how Ellen Spencer would hold up under it all. The good doctor, she decided, would probably just feed her a steady diet of pills to keep her numb.

The good doctor.

Maggie didn't trust him.

She'd put Charlotte Ramsey in charge of contacting Spencer's former associates in Greenwich as well as the hospitals where he'd been affiliated. She was also to check with nearby Methodist and see if Dr. Tom had been where he'd said he was on Saturday.

In a day or two, she'd know what was real and what wasn't.

She sighed, drawing her arm over her eyes, too tired to even get up and walk to her bedroom. She tucked her feet underneath her and curled in a ball, her head so heavy she couldn't think.

She drifted off.

A door creaked open.

A flash of light from the hallway broke through the room's darkness, and the little girl burrowed deep beneath her covers, hiding her face under the sheet.

She heard the click of the lock as the door was pushed shut, and the footsteps coming toward her, coming....

She closed her eyes as tight as she could, pretending she was as small as a speck of dust, too little to be seen.

Then the mattress dipped under his weight, and his hand tugged at the covers.

"Wake up, it's me."

The girl whimpered.

"Stop acting like baby."

His hand drew away the blanket, pulled the sheet to her ankles, despite how she cried to him, "Momma...I want my Mommy."

"Mommy's asleep. Besides, it's my turn to love you. Mommy loved you all day."

"Your love hurts."

He laughed at that. "Sometimes that's the price we pay." And then his voice turned harder, his hand settling on her leg.

She grabbed for the bedpost, but he caught her foot, jerking her toward him. She tried to scream, but his palm quickly smothered the sound, pushing down on her nose so that she couldn't breathe.

"Hush, now, you hear me? That's a girl. You know what'll happen if you make a noise and Mommy wakes up. She'll leave you like your daddy did. She'll go a thousand miles away."

His hand lifted off, and she gulped at the air, squirming as his fingers slid beneath her nightgown, catching in her

panties and pulling them down to her knees....
"No!"

Maggie bolted upright.

Disoriented, she looked around her.

The light from the kitchen filtered in, illuminating the green walls, the bookcases, the framed prints, and she got her bearings, remembered where she was.

She hugged herself. She was shaking.

It was getting to her, she knew. This case was gnawing at her from inside, dredging up things she didn't want to feel, hadn't felt in a long time.

She wiped at her eyes, brushing away the tears that had come as she'd slept.

"It's okay," she whispered to herself. "It's okay."

But a voice inside her head whispered back, "Is it? Is it really?"

Chapter Thirteen

The phone rang.

Maggie rolled over in bed, the covers twisted around her. Eyes cracked into slits, she glanced at the clock on her nightstand.

Not even half past six.

Jesus.

She bent the pillow over her ear and tried to ignore the damned noise. She'd had another near-sleepless night, and her head ached.

On the fourth ring, her machine caught it, and she heard a voice too chipper for so early asking, "Ryan? Ryan, hey, pick up would you?"

Phillips.

She groaned, but let the pillow flop away from her ear.

"Ryan, answer the damned phone. I got something you'll want to hear."

She rolled over and snatched up the receiver. "It's still

dark out," she growled at him, her voice gravel. She rubbed at her face, drawing herself up and against the wooden headboard.

"My youngest was up all night barfing her guts out. The wife was in and out of bed so much I couldn't sleep. So I thought I'd get an early start."

"You had to call to tell me that?" she said, but Phillips ignored her sarcasm.

"Got a copy of the ME's report."

"What?" She sat up straighter, suddenly wide awake, his announcement hitting her like a strong cup of coffee.

"Went by a half hour ago and picked it up myself. Your friend Mahoney was there," he said and paused, as if waiting for some response from her. When he didn't get it, he went on, "He told me himself that the body's already gone. The family had the funeral parlor pick it up late last night. Seems they're holding the service this morning, trying to get a leg up on the reporters."

Good luck, Maggie thought, remembering the crowd at the Spencers' house the day before. They'd find out somehow. They always did.

"Anyway, the report was hot off the press."

Maggie's heart raced. "What killed her?"

"Blunt trauma to the head. Soft tissue residue points to a brick. Her frontal lobe was crushed. Shattered it like glass."

Maggie remembered the welt near the little girl's hairline, the clotted blood and bluish cast, the opened eyes.

Had Carrie seen it coming?

She felt suddenly hot in the flannel of her pajamas. Her armpits were damp.

Carrie might've realized too late what was happening and had started to put up a fuss. Her mother had mentioned how bright she was, how stubborn and independent.

Maggie wondered if those traits might not have worked against Carrie in this case. He might not have killed her if she'd been quiet.

"You still there, Ryan?"

"I'm here."

"Could've fooled me," he said lightly, but then his tone turned serious. "She had a few recent hematomas around her mouth and nose."

"She must have yelled," Maggie whispered. "He tried to shut her up."

"Seems that way. Probably covered her mouth with his hand, caught her nose in the process, kid being so small and all. There were also bruises at her shoulders and arms consistent with him pinning her down."

"Any sign of ligature?"

"Nope. Her wrists and ankles were unmarked. No scrapes or burns. Nothing. Odd thing is, her sock was pretty clean. She'd lost the shoe, Ryan, but the sock was hardly dirty. He either carried her, or transported her across that field some-how."

Maggie nodded to herself, digesting every word.

"He killed her at the construction site. That's where the brick came from, best as we can tell. There were plenty of 'em lying around. And she had dust on her clothes and skin from the concrete foundation, not to mention minute particles from wood shavings and shit consistent with the site."

Maggie pictured someone leading Carrie from the park,

the little girl calm at first, talking to him, not knowing what was going on until she realized she was getting too far away from her mother and she panicked.

Had he gotten rough with her, his grip tighter on her shoulder, enough to scare her so that he forced his hand over her mouth? Had she fought him? Mahoney had mentioned a cut on her finger. Could that account for the blood stain on her sneaker? And then...what? Somehow, she'd lost her shoe to the dry grass, her ribbon to the breeze....

"Yo, Ryan."

His voice brought her thoughts back on track, and she held the receiver more tightly. "Was she sexually assaulted?"

"You mean penetration?"

"Yes." She waited for him to go on, afraid of what he was going to tell her, surprised at his answer.

"No, Maggie. He didn't rape her, not then anyway."

She rubbed at her eyes, but the ache behind them remained. "What the hell does that mean?"

"There wasn't any semen. No tearing. No indication that he'd even removed her clothes. But the report mentions some scarring in her anal cavity, which opens up the possibility that she'd been molested at some point earlier."

"How much earlier?"

"Weeks. Months. But it could mean nothing. Kids're constantly putting things in their mouths that are almost too big to shit, if you know what I mean. That might account for the scar tissue."

"Or it might not." Maggie pressed her forehead to the cool plastic of the receiver, closing her eyes, feeling sick to her stomach.

"Not much to go on, huh? Blood type on the shoe matches the victim's. Could be from the scratch on her finger, or else maybe it's his. Whoever took her." He paused, his loud voice turning soft. "Ryan? You fall asleep on me or something?"

She opened her eyes, pushing the receiver to her ear again. "I'm here," she said.

"The brass want to get a warrant to type Westmoreland. If he's O positive, then I'd say we're onto something even without the DNA results in our hands."

Except that 40% of the population is O positive, as Phillips himself had mentioned back in Sarge's office.

"Maybe," she said quietly, knowing that it wouldn't be enough. They had to have more, something solid and airtight. Hair or clothing fibers from Carrie in his car, a bite mark on a forearm with the imprint of Carrie's teeth. An eyewitness linking the two on that Saturday afternoon. Something. Anything.

The longer it took for them to find it, to find him, the more chance there was of physical evidence being destroyed, of them losing the scent. Of him getting away.

"You want a ride to the funeral?" he asked. "First Presbyterian at ten o'clock sharp."

"No," she said quietly. "I'll meet you there."

"You gonna be okay?" His voice turned gentle with concern, and she wondered if that's how he sounded when he talked to his girls.

"I will be," she said.

She sat where she was for a minute, rolling her head against the headboard, going over and over the possible scenarios, trying to piece together just what happened.

133

Carrie had known her abductor, had seen him before, had perhaps even trusted him. Maggie had never been more certain that he wasn't a stranger.

The construction site. Leonard said they'd found marijuana butts—roaches—scattered around, as if it were somebody's private hangout. The killer had been there before. He must have. The place wasn't picked randomly, it was selected because of its isolation, because the crew would have left by mid-afternoon on Saturday. It would've been deserted.

He might have intended only to molest her, and then to leave her there to wander home or be found when the crew came to work early Monday morning. Or he may have meant to return her to the park afterward, to pretend nothing had happened. Only he had killed her instead. He had covered up her body in the dumpster. Buried her with bricks.

This wasn't a random act of violence, though it might have been spur of the moment.

Her headache tweaked at her temples, and Maggie rubbed there with her fingertips.

She thought of all the videotapes she'd watched over and over again, all the still photographs she'd perused, all the phone tips that had led nowhere.

It didn't make sense, she thought. It didn't make sense.

Why hadn't anyone seen Carrie being led off from the park?

The soccer games were in progress. There were all kinds of people around.

She slumped beneath the covers.

Brian Westmoreland.

Could he have done it without rousing interest? But

wouldn't someone have remembered if he'd left after the game and taken her with him? Or were people used to seeing him with kids, so that no one had thought twice about it?

A man who worked with children, who was constantly surrounded by them, would not stand out if he drove off with a little girl in his car.

His car.

That was what didn't fit.

They had found her shoe and ribbon in a field that sat somewhere between the park and the construction site.

He couldn't possibly have driven across the pasture. No one had mentioned car tracks.

What if there was no car involved at all. And if they'd been on foot, why was there so little evidence of dirt on Carrie's sock? Had he carried her? Five miles was an awfully long walk. Maybe he'd ridden a bike.

She sighed, dropping her head to her knees. It had to be someone Carrie knew, and what if she didn't know Westmoreland?

Jake.

His name came to mind so abruptly, without her even thinking.

Maggie had been there when he'd come home the night of Carrie's disappearance. He'd looked dishevelled to say the least, shoes muddied, scrapes on his chin and hands. The police had picked him up a mile or so away, had put his mountain bike in the trunk. A bike he'd been riding all afternoon.

She wasn't convinced Jake had it in him. But she had been wrong before. Besides, gut feelings didn't hold up in a court of law. Evidence did.

She tossed about, restless, feeling as if there were something she was overlooking. Something she was missing.

She thought then of Ashley Vincent, of the frightened look on her face, the tears in her eyes as she'd stood on the steps in her tee-shirt, hair ruffled from her nap, her tiny voice as she'd told Tyler she wanted her mommy, that she was having nightmares during the day.

And Maggie knew she couldn't afford to make a mistake. She wouldn't be responsible for another child falling prey to a killer.

Chapter Fourteen

Someone was shaking her. Even through the fog in her head left over from her drug-induced sleep, Ellen felt the hand on her shoulder, jarring her awake.

"Get up, Ellen."

She peeled open her eyelids, blinking against the sunlight that swam through the parted drapes.

"It's nine o'clock." Tom's face hovered above her, features blurry. "You need to get moving."

She rolled over, away from him, closing her eyes, hiding beneath the covers. "Leave me alone," she whispered, her mouth dry, her tongue like cotton. "Go away."

"Ellen," he said, as if she were a child. He caught a handful of sheet and blanket and gave a yank, baring her. Then he grasped her by her shoulders.

She groaned, pushing ineffectually at him, balling her hands into fists. She had nothing to get up for, no reason to get out of bed. Carrie would never come home. Her baby was dead.

"Come on, pull yourself together. You look like hell. Why don't you get in the shower, okay? I'll give you something to take when you're dressed." He was pulling at her, dragging her off the mattress, despite her protests. Like an alcoholic drying out, she shook all over, her legs wobbling. Her teeth chattered, the noise like a jackhammer in her head.

She knew from the way he stared at her with pity in his eyes that she looked a fright. When he was young, he liked her hair mussed, liked her legs unshaven. He was so much more down-to-earth in those days. He had come to care so much of appearances, how everything seemed, how she looked, how she behaved.

She dropped her gaze to the floor, staring at her bare feet, at the chips in her red-painted toenails.

He sighed with impatience. "You've got to do this, Ellen. For Carrie, if not for me."

She raised her eyes slowly, taking in his polished Gucci loafers, the razor-sharp pleats of his black wool pants, at his button-down shirt, and his silk tie. His squared jaw was clean-shaven, but she saw the gray shadows below his eyes, the lines in his brow that seemed to have deepened these past few days.

"Hold me," she said, voice so small she wondered if he heard her. "Hold me."

"You get ready," he told her, touching her arm, but keeping her at a distance, "and I'll tend to Jake."

She could hardly move. She tried to inhale, sucking at the air, but it hurt even to breathe. Her limbs felt so heavy; her head gently drummed with a Valium hangover.

She went into the bathroom, leaned on the marble van-

ity, looked into the mirror, catching sight of someone she barely recognized. Thin angular face. Hollowed cheeks. Pale lips
and skin. Wounded eyes that stared back at her, so full of pain.

She turned away, peeling off her nightgown and panties
as the water from the shower pounded the tiles, filling her ears
with white noise. Steam rushed at her face as she stepped in
and let the water pelt her hard as hail, so hot she felt scalded,
but she didn't care. Every inch of her was battered and beaten,
inside and out. Nothing else could hurt her now. Nothing.

Every movement she went through was automatic.
Putting on her pantyhose, zipping up her black coatdress, slipping on her shoes, applying her makeup, fixing her hair.

She tried not to think of where she was going, because
she knew if she did, she might not make it through the day.

She was walking on a tightrope as it was, teetering
every inch of the way. And there was no net beneath her.

She needed some handkerchiefs and went over to
Tom's dresser where she kept them neatly pressed and folded
in his top left drawer.

Silver-framed photographs of the family, and of Tom
and Carrie alone, sat atop the maple bureau, and Ellen felt
drawn to them, reaching out to touch the smiling face of the little girl who'd once been hers.

A sob rushed up her throat, and she placed her hand
over her mouth, trying to stifle it.

It wasn't fair, she thought. It wasn't fair.

No one should have to bury their four-year-old child,
not like this.

She drew in a breath, her chest aching, and reached
shakily for the brass pull, sliding open the drawer to see the

neatly-laid socks, black with black, blue with blue, folded inside-out as her own mother used to do.

The handkerchiefs were neatly stacked on the right. Her fingers trembling, she snatched up several of the cotton squares. Something fell from between them, drifting down to the floor.

Ellen bent to pick it up.

"Oh, God."

A stream of pink trailed between her fingers.

Carrie's ribbon.

Her eyes widened as she stared.

It was one Carrie had worn to the park on Saturday, she'd tied it in her baby's hair.

Her heart thumped madly.

Had Tom removed it from the police evidence bag? Dear God, they'd said not to open them up, not to touch them.

She heard his footsteps in the hall, and quickly pushed the drawer closed, shoving the ribbon and the kerchiefs in her dress pocket. She turned around just as he walked through the door.

She opened her mouth, wanting to tell him what she'd found, to ask him why.

But she couldn't bring herself to do it.

"Here," he said and pressed a tiny yellow pill into her hand.

She took it without question, setting it on her tongue, hardly aware of its bitter taste. Tom then gave her a small glass of water and stood over her until she washed it down.

She wiped the back of her hand across her mouth, and he patted her cheek. "That should get you through the morning."

Her mother and father waited with Jake in the living room. They had arrived some time during the past forty-eight hours. She didn't know, for sure, when. Everyone looked so uncomfortable, tears welling in their eyes, hands trembling, that Ellen shut herself up, locked herself tight behind her frozen face.

Jake squirmed in his coat and tie. His hair appeared unwashed, and Ellen couldn't help thinking, why isn't he more like Carrie? He had never had her sweet nature, never had her bright laugh or vibrant smile. He had always been moody, withdrawing from her so that Ellen had turned her attentions away from him and to Carrie.

Tom got her coat and helped her into it, taking her arm as they went out of doors, down the stone path toward the long black limousine.

Several reporters had shown up again this morning, and Tom rushed her past the pack of them and into the back of the car.

She stared out the window as they drove, thinking of things that seemed so out of place.

Her graduation from college, the black robe she'd worn, the cap that would barely stay on her head.

Making love to Tom for the first time, legs intertwined, bodies hot, whispering words that she would never have said in the cold light of day.

Giving birth to Jake, the pain of it lasting nearly eight hours, the cry he'd let out when they'd slapped his bare bottom, the sound both frightening and thrilling.

Carrie clinging to her leg a month past when she and Tom had been heading out for dinner, her tiny voice pleading

141

with her not to go, and Ellen stroking her hair, telling her she'd be fine with Jake and Tyler, peeling off her tiny hands and walking away.

She saw, too, the child staring up at her from the table in the morgue, a face that was and wasn't Carrie's.

Tears slipped down her cheeks. She didn't bother to brush them away.

Carrie was gone. She would never again see her baby.

And it was her fault.

All her fault.

Tom touched her arm, and she started.

The car had pulled up in front of the church. Darkly-dressed people swarmed outside, far too many of them. Members of the media ringed the whitewashed building, and Ellen avoided them, fixing her eyes on the steeple.

The chauffeur opened the door, and Tom climbed out first, taking her arm as she followed.

Hands reached for her, voices called her name, faces peered at her from above raised collars and beneath hat brims.

Everything and everyone blurred together, the dull blues and blacks of clothing, the dirge-like music from the organ, the minister's cool touch as he clasped her fingers, whispering to her how sorry he was, that Carrie was in a better world now than this.

It was a dream.

Soon, she would wake up, and everything would be as it was again.

"This way, Ellen."

Tom urged her forward, up the aisle toward the tiny white casket with its spray of pink roses, and she stumbled on

the runner.
        He caught her arm, righting her.
        And she pulled away.

Chapter Fifteen

Maggie stood in back and watched the mourners file out, the organist playing a sad requiem until the church emptied.

The Spencers had left immediately following the service, hurrying from First Presbyterian with hardly a glance behind them. They were through the doors so quickly Maggie got only a glimpse of Ellen's tear-streaked face, but it was enough to break her heart.

So much for them keeping this quiet, she thought, recalling the crowds who'd shown up, so many that they'd had to station uniforms outside to keep away the overflow.

"You ready to go?"

She smoothed a hand over the buttons of her charcoal gray pantsuit, drawing in a slow breath as she turned to Phillips, he in a navy blue coat and striped tie. He wedged a finger between his collar and his throat, stretching his neck left and right.

"I can't breathe in this thing," he said through his

frown.

The packed church was overly-warm, the air thick with the smell of perfume and cologne, of artificial heat, and the too-sweet scent of flowers. Baskets of lilies and orchids, vases of roses, and wreaths of evergreen and mums covered the dais.

"Come on, Ryan. Show's over. Hi ho, hi ho, it's off to work we go." Phillips shrugged into the down-filled coat he'd held over his arm during the service. He reached for the black cloth coat Maggie had draped over her own arm, but she drew away.

"Go on ahead," she said. "I'll see you at the station."

His eyes on her narrowed below his thick brows. His forehead wrinkled. "You sure?"

She smiled thinly, patting his shoulder. "Go on, Dad, I'm fine."

He shook his head. "You're as stubborn as my own girls."

He walked off, glancing back at her before he pushed through the doors behind the last of the stragglers.

The organ music finally stopped, and, with the mourners gone, the church seemed all too quiet. The arched beams and high mud windows that shut out the sun made the empty space appear cavernous.

Maggie carried her coat and purse in her arms, and walked up the aisle slowly, hearing her own heartbeat as she went.

Images flashed through her mind. Another church, a different town. A gawky thirteen-year-old in a hand-me-down black dress standing beside her mother in the front pew. The older woman held a kerchief to her tear-damp cheeks as she gazed upon the opened casket on which a simple spray of mums rested. The girl stood quietly, staring upon the dead man's face, her eyes dry as a bone.

"Sad, isn't it?"

The voice startled Maggie.

A thin man in a black suit stepped out from behind one of the stone columns that rose to meet the arch above her head. He paused to gaze upon the coffin, his hands clasped at his waist.

He did not look at her as he spoke. "This has to be the worst part of the job. When little ones go. It just doesn't seem right, does it?" He bobbed his head as he surveyed the flowers and the casket. "Still, everything looks quite lovely, don't you think? The family said her favorite color was pink, so we arranged for the spray to be pink roses."

The funeral director, she realized, thinking then that their jobs weren't all that different in one respect. Each wanted to put the dead to rest.

Only for her it meant finding a killer.

Phillips was at his desk and on the phone when she got back to the station.

She hung her coat over her chair and tucked her purse into the bottom drawer, settling down at her desk.

There was a note from Greg Leonard stuck to a folder set atop a stack of files. "Don't know what you wanted this for. You into devil-worship and animal sacrifice these days? Kinky, Ryan, kinky."

What an ass, she thought and shook her head.

She flipped open the months-old file, setting aside everything else for the moment. She worked off the rubberband from a group of photographs which numbered about a dozen, then spread the pictures across her desk.

"Jesus!" She wrinkled her nose at the sight of the mutilated bodies of small dogs and cats, even a rabbit.

She didn't remember much about the case herself, as Leonard and Washington had headed up what there was of an investigation. Cutting up animals wasn't exactly considered serial killings, though it had made headlines in the local newspapers, playing on people's fears of satanic worship, animal sacrifices, and so forth. But the stories had as quickly dried up when the pet killings stopped and no suspect was found.

She gathered up the photographs and put them aside, drawing out the typed reports.

She scanned them once, then read them over more thoroughly, noting dates, addresses, names.

The animals had all been pets. The rabbit had been penned, the dogs fenced-in, the cats indoor/outdoor. The killings had occurred within about a five mile radius, the houses an easy walk or bike ride one from the other, which is why those Leonard and Washington had interviewed all thought a neighborhood kid had been involved.

"Everyone figured it was Jake...At least I did," she remembered Barbara Vincent telling her, though nothing in any of the reports mentioned Jake Spencer or any other suspect by name.

Jeffrey Dahmer had started out mutilating animals, she recalled, moving to human beings, experimenting with primitive lobotomies and cannibalism.

Serial killers often began practicing the art of murder as children. The family dog gets his throat slashed. The neighbor's cat is found hanging from a tree or drowned or with its neck broken.

Had someone in Litchfield's posh suburbs taken the next step from strangling Fido to murdering Carrie? She wondered, then shook off the idea.

She didn't want to believe that.

She was grasping at straws, wasn't she? Trying to link the unsolved pet killings to Carrie Spencer's death. It was a stretch by even her overtired imagination—but maybe not much of a stretch.

What they were dealing with here was a pedophile. She knew it in her gut, and Maggie had always trusted her instincts.

"Mind if I interrupt?"

She looked up to see Phillips leaning above her, hands braced on the edge of her desk.

"Be my guest," she said. "And it better be good news, or else I don't want to hear it."

"Okay," he said and started to leave.

"Phillips."

He turned around, wearing a slight grin.

She sighed. "Go ahead."

"The trace evidence found on Carrie Spencer's clothing isn't worth diddly. The fibers match the silk from her mother's warm-up suit, and the carpet fibers on the shoes and socks fit the pile and make of carpeting at the Spencer's house."

"Nothing that would suggest she'd been moved by car?"

"Sorry, Maggie." He tapped his fingers on her desk, looking no more happy than she felt, before he walked away.

Frustrated, she pushed aside the file on the pet killings and flipped open the manila folder that held information on

Kenny Wayne's disappearance in Pecan Creek.

"Detective, you have a minute?"

As always, Charlotte Ramsey had her hair pulled off her brow into a neat ponytail. A polished shield was pinned to the left breast of her dark blue uniform.

Maggie folded her arms over the papers and asked hopefully, "You got something for me?"

Ramsey nodded. "It's about Dr. Spencer. You wanted me to let you know what I found out from the hospital."

"Go on."

"I talked to the floor nurses at Methodist, the telephone operator, and a couple of the doctors who did time in the ER last Saturday."

Maggie leaned forward. "And?"

Charlotte pulled a small notepad from her breast pocket, flipping through it. "No one remembered seeing Dr. Spencer after about three on Saturday afternoon. He did show up in the ER that morning, at eight-fifteen, after they'd called him at home, and he made his rounds after that. A security guard named Hal Ketchum thought he saw Dr. Spencer's gray Mercedes pulling out of the employee lot about two-thirty, maybe quarter to three." Ramsey shrugged. "No one saw him again."

Tom Spencer had told her he'd gone across the street to his office to finish up paperwork. "They're sure he wasn't around? Methodist is a big place. He might've been in his office."

Ramsey shifted through her notes again. "One of his patients came into the ER with severe stomach pains at three o'clock. They paged Dr. Spencer over the hospital PA system for nearly thirty minutes, and they couldn't rouse him. His answering service tried the back line at his office repeatedly as well as his pager, but no cigar. They finally heard from him more than an hour later, just before he showed up at his residence on Woodlawn, from the sound of it. He apologized profusely, told them he didn't know he'd been beeped, that he might've turned off his pager by mistake."

Ramsey hesitated, tapping her chin with her notepad, her unlined face thoughtful. "They were pretty pissed that Spencer wasn't around. Another doctor had to cover for him, a Frank Hiler." She grinned suddenly, and her plain features brightened. "He said Spencer owes him big."

Maggie pushed away from her desk, tilting back in her chair. She shook her head. It didn't make sense. Where was Tom Spencer for more than an hour? Why was he so hard to reach? If he had accidentally shut off his pager, then why hadn't he told her as much? Embarrassment? Or was it an out and out lie. Maggie couldn't see Tom Spencer doing anything without reason. She doubted there was much in his life left to fate.

She looked up at Ramsey. "Anything on Connecticut?"

Ramsey rolled her eyes heavenward and sighed. "Talk about a good ol' boys' network. Everyone's as tight-lipped as can be at the hospital where Dr. Spencer practiced. I have a few more names to follow-up, a nurse that recently retired, and I'm waiting for a call from the DA's office, in case there was anything like malpractice that sent him running." She cocked her head. "Is that it?"

"Will you do one more thing for me? Well, two really."

The young woman's eyes lit up. "Sure, Maggie. You name it."

"Check with the Spencers' phone company, would you? See if you can trace where he was when he called back to the hospital."

"So what's number two?"

"Get in touch with Methodist again, and find out Tom Spencer's blood type."

Ramsey shoved her notepad into her breast pocket. "I'll get on it right now, Detective."

"Thanks."

She hurried off, leaving Maggie to ponder just where the hell Tom Spencer was on Saturday around the time his daughter vanished. Because he wasn't where he said he was, that much was clear.

Her phone rang, making her jump, and she reached to snatch it up.

"Maggie Ryan."

Silence filled her ear, so she tried again.

"Hello?"

"Detective Ryan?" The voice sounded like a child's. Breathless. "It's Ellen Spencer."

Maggie's chest constricted, and she found herself speechless.

"I need to see you." The words slurred together, like someone drunk or on tranquilizers. "I found something I want to show you," she went on in hushed tones, a sob breaking her up before she finished, "It's about Carrie. Can you come to the house?"

"I'm on my way." Maggie said, reaching for her purse.

Chapter Sixteen

"Anything new, Detective?" A petite brunette shoved a microphone in her face as Maggie got out of her car.

"We're pursuing several leads," she said tersely and proceeded across the lawn toward the Spencers' front door.

One hand on her purse, she ducked her chin into the collar of her coat, hoping they'd leave her alone. But, she figured, that was like asking rain not to be wet.

"We heard you've got a suspect under surveillance," a male voice interjected, and Maggie hesitated, her step faltering. They knew about Westmoreland.

"Is it true, Detective?"

She turned toward a slightly-built man with long gray hairs combed across his pink pate.

"We're following up several leads," she repeated, not about to give him anything to play upon, to embellish for the evening news. They listened in on police scanners, they showed up where they weren't wanted, and distorted the truth

152

so often that she wondered if they knew what it was anymore.

She tried to figure how long it would be before they lost interest in this case. When Carrie's killer was caught? Or when another more sordid murder took precedence?

To her it seemed a harsh way to earn a living, but then, the reporters might say the same of what she did.

At least I try to catch the sons-of-bitches who do the killing, she mused, instead of glorifying them and giving them attention they don't deserve.

"If you'll excuse me," she said, pulling away from the persistent few who tagged alongside her, though they still shouted questions at her even when she'd turned her back.

She walked up to the door and rang the bell. A shadow fell cross the peephole, and the door was drawn open about a foot.

Tom Spencer barred her entrance with his arm. He was wearing the dark suit she'd seen him in at the funeral, though he'd removed the jacket and loosened his tie. He made no move to invite her in. "What the hell are you doing here?"

"Your wife called..." Maggie began.

But Ellen appeared in the foyer, explaining for her, "I asked her to come."

Tom dropped his arm away, moving toward Ellen. Maggie slipped through the door, closing it behind her.

Ellen had not changed out of her funeral clothes either, though her black coatdress looked rumpled. She'd removed her shoes and stood in her stocking feet while her husband fussed at her.

"Goddammit, Ellen." He took hold of her shoulders and looked into her eyes. "You should be resting. Do you need another tranquilizer?"

She brushed at his hands. "I'm not an invalid, Tom. Don't treat me like one."

It was the first time Maggie had heard her speak up to him, and she was surprised by the strength in Ellen's voice, despite its weariness.

"I only want to help." Tom softened his approach, though there was still an edge of impatience in his tone. "You shouldn't overtax yourself."

Ellen ignored him, nodding at Maggie. "Follow me," she said, crossing to the curving staircase, her footsteps muted by the pile carpet that ran seamlessly upward.

Tom called after her, "Ellen?"

But she didn't stop, and Maggie stayed right behind her.

They passed the playroom still scattered with Carrie's toys. Dust particles danced in the light that beamed in through the windows, lending an air of neglect. Maggie figured it would be a long while before Ellen would gather up the strength to pack it all away, the dolls, the games, the soft stuffed animals.

She followed Ellen to Carrie's room, wondering what this was about, why Tom Spencer had not been invited to join them.

"I came up today...after the service." Ellen talked as she walked around, touching the bedpost, the desk, the chair, the lamp shade—as if performing some strange dance. "Tom thought I was napping."

Maggie unfastened the top button on her coat. It felt so warm in here.

"I wanted to feel her with me," Ellen went on, her back

to Maggie. "I needed to be with her again...oh, God." She stopped, her shoulders shook.

Maggie started to move, to go to her, but held herself back. There was nothing she could do to comfort Ellen Spencer. A touch wouldn't suffice, and no words were good enough.

It was another minute before Ellen straightened up, pushing a hand against the air as if to signal to Maggie that she was all right again.

She went over to a small wooden chest painted with ballet slippers, bending to lift the lid, and removing papers rolled up with a rubberband.

Clutching them to her breasts, she faced Maggie. "I found these," she said, not looking at all happy about it. "I'd never seen them before."

She took them to the desk and laid them out, pressing them flat, though they curled up on the ends. She switched on the ballerina lamp to cast bright light upon them.

Maggie went over.

"Carrie drew them," Ellen told her, smoothing trembling fingers over the crayon-covered construction paper. "But she never showed them to me," she said in a hoarse whisper. "She must have hidden them on purpose. She'd never done that before. Hidden something from me, I mean."

Maggie stared at the dark slashes and circles, the almost angry-looking streaks of black and blue and red. Too bleak, she would have thought, for a child's hand. There was no brightness, no use of softer hues.

"This is her, isn't it? This is Carrie." Ellen dragged her fingers over a simply-drawn face, large blue teardrops falling from the eyes, the mouth an upside down curve. Above this was a stick figure, black slashes for arms and legs, the head colored mask-like with black crayon.

She slid another page out from beneath the first one, the drawing similar, though this time there were two stick figures hovering, one with his head shaded in, the other with pin-dot eyes and a frown.

"What does it mean?" Ellen asked, and there was urgency in her voice.

Maggie could venture a guess, but she wasn't about to. "Can I take them? I'd like to show them to a friend of mine who's a therapist. She deals with children."

Ellen blinked tear-glazed eyes and nodded.

Maggie rolled up the drawings and fastened them together with the rubberband. She slipped her leather bag off her shoulder onto the small desk and pulled it open, shifting its contents so she could get the drawings in with only a couple inches protruding.

She couldn't help thinking about the ME's report, about the findings of scar tissue in Carrie's anal tract. Whether it was her job to be suspicious or her nature, she couldn't keep from speculating that Carrie may have been molested, that such abuse might very well be at the root of her death.

And now there were these images Carrie had drawn.

Maggie wanted some answers.

She turned to Ellen. "I need to talk to you, Mrs. Spencer. About your husband."

"Tom?" Ellen fiddled with the buttons on her coatdress.

"He called me yesterday at the station."

Her cheeks flushed. "Did he tell you about the ribbon

then? Did he give you an explanation. Oh, God, I was so worried. I'm sure he didn't mean to take it."

Maggie had no idea what she was talking about. "The ribbon?"

"He's not in trouble, is he? For not telling you sooner?"

"I'm sorry, I don't understand."

She was starting to look scared. "The pink ribbon I found in his bureau drawer this morning. I thought he took it from the plastic bag, even though you said not to open them. He did mention it?"

"No, he didn't." Maggie's mind jumped ahead of her as it always did, trying to figure out what Ellen meant. She knew for a fact that the ribbon found by the K-9 unit wasn't missing. The forensics lab had just returned it the day before, and Maggie had logged it into the evidence locker herself.

"I...I took it from his drawer," Ellen stammered, reaching into her pocket. She fished out a strip of pink and handed it to Maggie. "I didn't know what he'd done...how he got it."

Maggie stared at the grosgrain ribbon pinched between her fingertips, and her neck prickled.

This was it, she knew. The twin to the one they'd picked up from the field several miles from the park.

When Carrie's body was recovered from the dumpster, she'd had only elastic bands in her pigtails. The matching ribbon had been missing. Until now.

"He's not in trouble, is he?"

"I don't know." If the ribbon proved to be the other's mate, he was in big trouble, she thought, but didn't say as much to Ellen. At the very least, tampering with evidence came to mind, as did obstruction of justice. "We'll see what happens."

Ellen moaned.

Maggie dropped the ribbon into her coat pocket, hoping to hell it wouldn't burn a hole in the cloth.

Jesus, what was going on?

She looked around her, at the canopied bed that would stay empty, at the books on the shelves that would never be read, and she wondered if Tom Spencer knew far more about his daughter's death than he was telling.

Ellen rubbed her arms and turned away. She went over to the bed and sat down, hugging a carved post. "Are you very close to finding who did it?" she asked, her voice raw.

Maggie didn't lie. "We may be." They had a suspect, anyway, which was more than they had forty-eight hours ago, and Brian Westmoreland fit the type. But the case itself was far from closed. The pink ribbon just added another layer of complexity.

"Is there something more I can do to help?"

"Are you up to answering some questions?" Maggie asked, more than ready to take her offer to heart.

Ellen touched her forehead to the bedpost, her reply slow to come. Finally, she nodded. "If it will help Carrie."

"Are you sure?"

"Yes."

Maggie started out with what she thought was something simple. "Can you tell me why you left Connecticut?"

Ellen glanced up, surprise in her eyes. "I don't see what that has to do with anything that's gone on here."

Her expression told Maggie exactly what her answer didn't. That something had happened in Greenwich, something that had forced them to go. Something unpleasant.

158

"Was it because of your husband? Did it have to do with his practice?"

Ellen fidgeted, avoiding her eyes. "Tom got a wonderful offer here with Methodist, that's all."

Her body language said otherwise. "Please be honest with me, Mrs. Spencer. I'll find the answer soon enough, either way. I've got someone checking with the hospital in Greenwich. They're in touch with the staff there and with the DA's office..."

"Someone checking?" Ellen looked and sounded afraid. "Oh, God." She drew her hands between her knees, dropping her head. "Oh, God."

Maggie went to her, crouching down and reaching out for her hand, willing Ellen to meet her eyes. "Please," she urged as gently as she was able. "I need to know."

Ellen turned away, letting out a sob that shook her. Still, Maggie held on. "There was some trouble," she whispered, and Maggie bent nearer to hear. "Tom said it was all a mistake. A misunderstanding."

"What kind of misunderstanding?"

"With some of his patients." As she talked, she glanced at the door, grasping Maggie's hand and leaning on the bedpost. "They threatened him with malpractice. They said he...that he was inappropriate with them."

"Sexually?"

She blushed. "Yes."

"Any children involved?"

She reared her head. "Dear God, no. Tom would never...he said they were crazy...that it was in their minds, that's all." She quieted suddenly and pressed her lips together,

159

as if she'd said too much.

"Was your husband"—Maggie paused, Ellen's wounded eyes watching her, knowing there was no easy way to say this—"did Carrie ever suggest to you that her father touched her in a sexual manner?"

"What?"

"Was she frightened of him?"

"No," Ellen's answer was quick, heartfelt. "Carrie loved her daddy."

"The medical examiner found some scarring that's suspicious."

"Stop it." Tears filled Ellen's eyes. "Just stop it."

Maggie rose from her crouch. "I didn't mean to offend you."

Ellen didn't respond.

Lay off, Maggie, she told herself, realizing she'd pushed Ellen enough. For God's sake, she'd just buried her daughter this morning.

"I'll let myself out," she said.

She was at the bedroom door when she heard the hushed, "Detective."

She stopped where she was.

"Whatever he did, Tom loved Carrie very much. He would never have hurt her. Never."

There was such desperation in her face and in her voice that Maggie wanted to believe her.

But she couldn't.

Not yet.

Maggie went downstairs, pausing at the base of the steps, hearing voices coming from the direction of the kitchen. She breathed in the smell of coffee, warm and cinnamon, and figured Carrie had felt safe here. This was the kind of place where you were supposed to feel protected.

She tried to picture how it must have been before this all happened. Rock music filtering down from Jake's stereo, probably turned up too loud, Carrie's laughter tickling the air, *Sesame Street* on the television.

One day had changed everything, and they could never go back.

Her beeper went off, scattering her thoughts, and she turned her head.

Tom Spencer stood in the middle of the foyer, staring at her. She hadn't even heard his footsteps.

She shut off her pager, looking over at him. "Can I use your phone?"

"Take it in the den," he said calmly, almost in monotone, nothing like the broken-voiced man who'd phoned her yesterday.

She held his eyes for a moment, and her hand went to her coat pocket, knowing what was inside. She wanted badly to confront him then and there. But it was too soon; she didn't have what she needed. Besides, she knew, the lies he'd told would trap him soon enough.

"Thank you," she said and pushed away from the newel post, heading toward the den.

She felt him watching her even as she walked away from him, toward the room where she'd met Ellen, where Phillips had first shown her a picture of Carrie.

The telephone was on the desk, and she picked up the receiver. She thought she heard a faint click as if someone had picked up the extension, but maybe it was just her imagination.

She dialed Phillip's cell phone, asking, "What's up?"

"Maggie?" His voice sounded breathless, excited, and her stomach clenched. Something was up indeed. "It's going down, Ryan, now."

"What?"

"Westmoreland. He tried to pack his bags and slip out. He must be scared as hell to want to run. But our boys were on him before he'd gone a mile. They stopped him for a broken tail-light, and, damned if he didn't put up a fuss." Phillips laughed. "Looked all wild-eyed, they said. So they made him get out, while they hand-searched his car." He stopped, and she could hear someone else talking to him. Then he was back. "You there, Ryan?"

"Yes."

"They found more than just a suitcase in his trunk. He had a teddy bear, would you believe it, and a beat-up old doll. Oh, and a dog's leash. There was also a roll of duct tape, and what they think may be some dried blood near the tirewell."

"Shit." She could hardly breathe.

"Sarge got a search warrant from Judge Landers. We're at his place now."

A teddy bear, a doll, and a dog's leash in his trunk, she thought, the hair at her nape standing up. A pedophile's lures. Had he used them with Kenny Wayne, and with Carrie as well?

"Creekside Apartments on Swallowtail," he barked, and she nodded to herself as he added, "Get over here, would you? You're missing all the fun."

And Then She Was Gone

"I'm gone," she told him, hanging up. She rushed from the house, wondering all the while if this was it. If it was over.

Chapter Seventeen

A handful of blue-and-whites and several unmarked cars she recognized were parked at Building B of the Creekside Apartments when Maggie pulled up.

People gawked from their doorways, watching wide-eyed, no doubt wondering what the hell was going on.

Maggie climbed up the concrete steps of an uncovered stairwell to an apartment with a uniformed officer standing guard just outside a paint-peeled door.

She pulled out her leather wallet from her purse, hooking it over the belt so that her shield was clearly visible.

He nodded and let her pass.

She went inside to find half a dozen cops crowding the small apartment. Beneath her feet was tattered brown carpet and around her were beige walls marred with holes from pictures hung by former tenants. Westmoreland had apparently not put up any of his own.

This complex was at least ten years old, she figured,

lower rent than the newer, more fashionable ones that had sprung up across Litchfield during the past year's building craze.

She heard cabinets being opened then shut again; voices conversing as the search was conducted.

She picked her way through the living room, sidestepping cushions pulled from a couch and matching chairs in a plaid that had "rental" written all over them. Drawers were upended, their sparse contents removed. Brian Westmoreland hadn't accumulated much since his arrival in Litchfield a couple weeks before. Perhaps he'd never intended to stay long, just time enough to molest a few kids at the YMCA, before he packed up and moved somewhere else to start over.

She peered up a narrow hallway and saw a closet door standing wide, a woman in blue going through it inch by inch.

"Good, you're here."

Phillips came up beside her and, taking her arm, shepherded her out of the mess cluttering the small living room and into the bedroom beyond where still more officers worked.

He led her over to the bed, which had been stripped. Atop the bare mattress lay an untidy pile of magazines.

Phillips picked up a few and held them out to her. "Take a look at his reading material. Shakespeare it ain't."

Penthouse and *Screw*, she noted, unable to disguise the disgust in her voice as she commented, "I'll bet he buys them for the articles."

Phillips snorted. "Yeah, right, and he gets these here just for their artistic value." He had tossed the magazines down and grabbed up several others.

Maggie took them from him. She stared at them, a bitter taste flooding her mouth.

"Looks like our zebra didn't change his stripes after all," Phillips remarked. "Homemade, don't you think? He must still have a pipeline somewhere or else he makes his own."

Maggie looked down at the pages in horror, feeling worse than sick.

Children.

None older than ten.

None were clothed.

All of them were engaged in sex acts that made Maggie's stomach curl.

She couldn't look at any more, and dropped the magazines with a groan. Her eyes clouded, and she closed them, trying to keep herself in control.

"Would you believe he'd hidden them under the mattress, like a kid squirrelling away a stolen copy of Daddy's *Playboy*?"

Maggie shook her head, opening her eyes, running fingers through her hair, ignoring their slight tremble. "Are they holding him on suspicion?"

Phillips swung his hands before him, gently slapping them together. "He's as good a suspect as they come." He hit his fist against his palm as he uttered, "Motive, means, and opportunity, Ryan. He had all three. Not to mention a criminal record for molesting children."

She turned away from the bed, walking over to a window. She looked out, staring down at a loaded dumpster. How fitting, she mused, for trash like Brian Westmoreland to gaze down upon garbage.

Phillips came up beside her. "Don't tell me you think

he's innocent?"

"Innocent?" Maggie scoffed. "Hardly. I figure it's way too much of a coincidence that he was staying with his sister in Pecan Creek when Kenny Wayne disappeared."

Phillips nodded, his sun-baked wrinkles framing his eyes and the thin line of his mouth. "We've already notified Pecan County. Sheriff's on his way."

She nodded, rubbing her arms, wondering if they had any luck showing Westmoreland's picture around Pecan Creek, sure that the sheriff wouldn't be driving over so quickly if they hadn't turned up something.

"They're gonna' get a confession out of him, Ryan, one way or another. Sarge thinks we've got our man, and I'm inclined to agree."

Maggie didn't respond. She watched the reflection of a young blond-haired officer in the bureau mirror as he rifled through dresser drawers.

"You're not so sure he killed Carrie Spencer. Are you Maggie?"

She told him the truth. "I don't know."

"Christ." He stalked halfway across the small room, then doubled-back to her, hands in the air. He leaned toward her, face flushed, asking in a low voice, "What kind of proof do you need? This guy's a fucking pervert. A bonafide child molester that some idiot parole board cut loose early because he was such a model convict. Kept his cell clean and made damned fine license plates to boot."

His sarcasm made her flinch. She wasn't used to this from Phillips. Unlike Greg Leonard and some of the others, he listened to her opinions and never chided her for what she felt.

He'd always told her to listen to her gut, which was exactly what she was doing.

She knew deep inside that this wasn't meant for her; he wanted this guy put away for good.

And so did she.

"I think," she said softly, "that Westmoreland did in fact murder a child."

"And if he confesses to two?"

She forced herself to smile. "Hey, I'm a good guy, remember?"

"Okay," he said, backing off. "I'm sorry."

She didn't tell him about the ribbon, didn't much feel like talking with him now at all.

There was nothing more for her to do, so she left the apartment. Phillips followed her out into the parking lot.

He leaned through her opened window as she belted herself in. "I almost forgot," he said while she stabbed her key into the ignition. "We didn't have to get a warrant to type Westmoreland's blood. Parole board gave us what we wanted." His eyebrows arched, and he looked unusually smug. "He's O positive, in case you're interested. Just like the stain on Carrie Spencer's shoe."

Chapter Eighteen

Maggie took the highway into northernmost Dallas, exiting at Preston, then followed Harvest Hill until she reached the familiar office complex near the Tollway.

She left her car in the parking garage and took the elevator up to the third floor. The office she wanted was at the end of a long hall, the door marked discreetly, "Terry Fitzhugh, CSW-MSW."

Maggie let herself into a waiting room cluttered with plastic blocks and coloring books.

A young woman with cropped red hair glanced up behind a window of sliding glass, which she quickly pushed aside. "Can I help you?" she said on cue, then her round face broke into a smile. "Oh, Maggie, hi. Terry's in the back with a patient."

"Can she spare a minute?"

"I think she can squeeze you in between sessions."

"Thanks, Cathy."

"No problem."

Maggie settled into a chair and set her purse in her lap. She removed the rolled-up drawings and balanced them on her knees.

The table beside her was covered with children's magazines. A lone copy of *People* with Madonna on the cover seemed oddly out of place.

Framed finger paintings covered cranberry-colored walls, the work of Terry's son, Andy.

"Almost makes you want to have a rug rat of your own, doesn't it?" Cathy said from the receptionist's window, and Maggie realized the girl had been watching her. "Terry's a great mother, isn't she?"

Maggie nodded and glanced away, hardly in the mood for small talk.

Cathy seemed to take the hint and slid the window closed again. Even so, Maggie heard the gentle click of a computer keyboard through the glass, and she relaxed a bit, sitting in an overstuffed chair, resting her head against the wall.

She let her eyes close, thinking of Westmoreland, of his arrest, and of the pink ribbon in her pocket. Fatigue rolled in like a fog, and she must've dozed off for a moment. At the pop of an opening door, she jerked awake and looked up to find Terry standing there, a quiet smile on her lips. "Maggie," she said, "Come on back."

Maggie gathered up her things and followed after her friend, up a narrow hallway decorated with more framed finger paintings and into an office with a wall of windows, the light filtered out by fabric-covered shades. Books crammed each of the dozens of built-in shelves, though small stuffed animals had been propped up incongruously amidst the myriad of professional texts.

Terry motioned her toward the burgundy sofa, its cushions broken up by needlepoint pillows in floral designs that picked up the green and blue in the Oriental rug underfoot.

Setting aside her purse, Maggie hung onto the drawings. She didn't even unbutton her coat. Terry plunked down beside her and arranged her brown wool dress over her crossed legs. A beaded necklace glittered at her collar.

"I take it this isn't a social visit?"

"I wish it were," Maggie admitted. She removed the rubberband and spread the papers across the coffee table, pushing aside a doll with all her private parts enlarged absurdly.

"Sorry," Terry said and leaned over to scoop up the doll, tucking it into the cushions.

Maggie used a ceramic ashtray to help pin down the curled construction paper.

"Okay"—Terry rubbed her hands together—"what've you got for me?"

"They were drawn by the four-year-old girl who was murdered. Carrie Spencer," she said. "Her mother found them. Apparently, she'd never seen them before. Carrie had hidden them."

"Let's take a look." Terry bent over the pictures, saying nothing at first, her dark eyes flitting back and forth as she took it all in. She reached out to touch the slashes of color, seeing things that Maggie knew she herself couldn't see.

"You're afraid she may have been abused," she said after her long silence.

"Yes."

Terry released a held breath. "It's hardly scientific, you know, interpreting what children draw. It's a little like the Rorshach blots, isn't it? You might see something very different from what I see."

"But you do see something, don't you?"

Terry faced her, the fine-boned features solemn, the slim brow wrinkled. "These aren't happy pictures with flowers and birds and kitties. There's darkness here. And fear."

It wasn't what Maggie had wanted to hear, but it was what she'd expected.

"It's possible she felt threatened in a sexual manner," Terry said and pointed to one of the stick figures. "This one appears to have a penis, doesn't he? And she blacked-out his face. The other one seems to be watching. God, Maggie, I don't know." She shook her head. "It's impossible to understand the implications without talking to the child. Which, in this case, we can't do."

Maggie didn't agree. She thought she knew what Carrie had implied with her crayons. She felt she knew exactly what had frightened her.

"Is there any evidence she'd been molested?"

"The ME found some scarring in her anal cavity."

Terry frowned. "Did you bring this up with the child's mother?"

"She categorically denies anyone had ever hurt the child."

"But you don't believe her?"

"I don't trust him."

"Who?"

"The father."

Terry eyed her, as if she wanted to ask a question.

Maggie busied herself with rolling up the drawings and securing them with the rubberband. She pushed them back into her purse.

"You want to talk?" Terry touched her arm. "I haven't seen you so worn out since you left the DPD."

"I haven't had a case like this since then," Maggie said quietly, trying to breathe when the room felt so warm, the air so stuffy. "I'm having nightmares...I can't go to sleep without seeing her...feeling him...Jesus." She squinted toward the blinds; she could make out the gray arms of barebranched trees through the slits. "And then Momma...she keeps calling..." her voice broke, and she stopped, knowing she was losing it. She swallowed hard and tried to compose herself.

"It's all right." Terry rubbed Maggie's arm. "It's all right to feel this way..."

"No." She got up slowly, and Terry's hand dropped away. "No, it isn't."

"Don't do this, Maggie."

She ignored Terry's plea, picking up her purse and slipping it over her shoulder.

Terry stood. "You can't shut it off..."

"Yes," Maggie whispered, "I can."

She had to. She had no choice. It was how she'd gotten through each day, and how she'd get through each day until Carrie's killer was caught.

She could take care of herself later.

173

She found Phillips at his desk back at the station.

"They've had Westmoreland in there for almost an hour," he told her, his eyes lit up. "Sheriff Moody's in with Sarge, working him over. Seems his deputies took Westmoreland's mug shot around Pecan Creek, showed it to everyone who lived or worked within ten miles of where Kenny Wayne was abducted. Some old guy who runs a gas station remembered a man who matched Westmoreland's description filling up his tank the same day the boy disappeared. They got a credit card slip with his sister's name on it, but the signature's his. According to Moody, the old man mentioned Westmoreland appeared kind of out of it. Like he was high or on something. But otherwise, he didn't pay him much attention. Said he looked like your average doped-up kid."

Maggie shifted her gaze to her bulletin board across the way, where Kenny Wayne's photograph smiled back at her alongside Carrie's.

"The gas station's maybe a mile from the Wayne's place, and there isn't a heck of a lot in between. Moody says it's mostly farm and pastureland. The Wayne's house is pretty isolated. It would've been a piece of cake for him to take the boy without being seen."

Maggie fingered her coat buttons, trying to assimilate it all, to make sense of it.

"He's guilty as hell, Ryan."

She nodded. "I agree. I think he murdered Kenny Wayne and dumped his body."

"But you still don't believe he murdered Carrie Spencer, do you?" he asked, his voice low.

"I'm not convinced, no."

"C'mon, Maggie!" He hit his hand against his desk, rattling a mugfull of pencils. "He's a convicted pedophile, right? This is what he does. It's his thing." He was breathing hard, his face flushed all the way up from his collar, and she could smell his sweat, his frustration. "He's our man. I know he is. He kidnapped and killed the boy from Pecan Creek, and then he moved to Litchfield and did the same to Carrie Spencer."

She looked at him, at the conviction in his eyes, and said, "I hope you're right."

"I am," he insisted, then he got up from his chair and brushed past her.

Maggie watched him as he strode between the crowded desks, until he passed through the doorway and was gone.

Something heavy pressed down on her shoulders, weighing her down. Her eyes burned, and she struggled not to let it pull her under.

She went over to her desk and took her coat off, digging the ribbon from her pocket. Then she sealed the strip of pink grosgrain in an envelope and dated it, marking "Received from E. Spencer" on its face. She wanted to check it against the pink ribbon in evidence, see if they matched without question, before she turned this one in and implicated Carrie's father in her murder.

"Maggie? You got a sec?"

She put the envelope inside her top drawer, as Charlotte Ramsey hovered above her desk wearing an eager expression.

"I got hold of the DA in Greenwich."

"Yes?"

"Looks like three women had filed charges of misconduct against Tom Spencer last year." The young officer shifted from foot to foot in the ugly black shoes that were regulation. "They claimed he'd behaved inappropriately with them during routine exams. The DA says they were all separate cases. The women were strangers, two in their twenties, one barely fifteen."

Maggie whispered, "Jesus."

"Charges were dropped pretty abruptly it seems. Dr. Spencer's partners got them to settle out of court for undisclosed sums." She twisted her ponytail round and round her finger before dropping it altogether. "I did speak with that retired nurse I told you about. She used to work with Dr. Spencer and told me, off the record of course, that she heard on the grapevine that his partners hooked him up with the job at Methodist. Helped him to get his Texas license to practice here. They wanted him as far away as they could get him."

Sexual misconduct with a teenage girl, Maggie thought, wondering why the hell the DA hadn't pressed harder to make the charges against him stick.

Undisclosed sums.

She rubbed at her temples, feeling anger. Money talks, she thought.

"Detective Ryan?"

"Sorry, Charlotte. Anything else?"

"Just a couple things. Apparently when Dr. Spencer finally returned the hospital page, he used his mobile phone. The phone company can only say it was made from somewhere within their coverage area."

"Which means?"

"Almost anywhere in Litchfield."

"Can't they get more specific?"

Ramsey grinned. "They said they'd work on it."

Maggie sighed. "Great."

"I did talk to the blood bank at Methodist. Dr. Spencer gave a pint last month. They said he's A positive."

Another common type, but it didn't match the stain on Carrie's sneaker. Still, it didn't rule him out as a suspect.

Or Westmoreland, she thought, remembering what Phillips had told her earlier this afternoon. If only the damned DNA tests didn't take weeks.

"Is there anything else...?"

"No," Maggie said, looking up at Ramsey's anxious face. "You've done a great job. Thanks."

Charlotte blushed and walked off, her back ramrod straight.

Maggie pushed away from her desk and got up, leaving the squad room. She crossed the hallway and approached the observation room, entering as quietly as she was able.

Heads turned as she closed the door behind her. She ignored their glances and settled into a folding chair next to Phillips, glancing at him for a second and then fixing her gaze dead-ahead at the one-way window.

Sheriff Moody sat knee to knee with Westmoreland, who slouched down in his chair, clearly exhausted. Phillips had said they'd already been on him for nearly an hour, and it showed. Westmoreland looked beaten.

Sarge was relentless, pacing a circle around them, arms wildly gesturing, his face red, eyes ablaze.

"...you spotted her during the soccer game, didn't you? Thought she was a pretty thing. Made you feel extra good, didn't it. Maybe she'd wandered across the park by then, and when the games ended, with all the kids running around and no

177

one paying you the least attention, you went over to Carrie, got her to leave with you, then you took her to the empty house and tried to rape her..."

"No," Westmoreland was saying, shaking his head, his chin rolling on his chest. "No, that's not what hap...."

"C'mon now, son," Sheriff Moody cut him off. "We all know what you are. We've got forensics checking out your car right now. They found blood stains in your trunk, you know that, boy?"

Brian's chin jerked up.

"They got them some hair fibers, too. Oh, and a roll of duct tape." The sheriff leaned toward him. "All the evidence'll prove you took Kenny Wayne, that you killed him. You wanna' make it easier on yourself, don't you?" His southern-boy drawl turned softer, as if he pitied Westmoreland, wanted to help him. "Now, tell us where you left the body, son. That's all we want you to do."

Westmoreland put his hands over his face, kept shaking his head. "I have rights," he mumbled over and over. "I won't say a word without a lawyer."

Sheriff Moody countered his protests with, "Son, what the hell's a lawyer gonna' do for you when we've got all the evidence?"

Maggie couldn't even see Westmoreland's face, his head hung so low.

Sarge stepped up behind Westmoreland and gripped the back of his chair, shaking it so that Brian jumped. "You're a three time convicted child molester! No attorney worth his salt's gonna' want to go down on a sinking ship. You think any jury in their right mind's gonna; set you free? No chance in hell, kid, not when they know about Pecan Creek, not when they see the crime scene pictures of Carrie Spencer. You get what I'm saying now? You're going rot in prison for the rest of your goddamned life!"

Brian's head shot up. "I didn't kill her! You can't pin that on me!"

"But you killed Kenny Wayne, didn't you, boy?" Sheriff Moody said, his head so near to Brian that their noses nearly touched. "You may as well confess it, 'cause the forensics people're gonna know soon enough that you had the boy in your car. Gas station attendant's signed a statement he saw you less than a mile from the boy's house that same afternoon." He put a hand on Brian's shoulder. "C'mon now, son, you're making this a helluva lot harder than it has to be."

There was a moment of quiet when no words were spoken, and Maggie felt as if they'd gone too far. That all of it was for nothing.

Then he started to sob.

Westmoreland broke down, his shoulders rocking.

"He's like all of them," Greg Leonard said from behind her, his voice hushed. "He's not sorry for a minute that he did it, but sorry as hell he got caught."

Maggie turned to find Phillips watching her, his face strained, but triumphant.

She'd suddenly had enough and got up, letting herself out of the room, thinking of Carrie's killer and wondering if anyone would believe her if she told them they had the wrong man.

Chapter Nineteen

They found Kenny Wayne the next morning.

Brian Westmoreland had told them where to look. The boy's body had been dumped in a ditch that ran alongside unfenced pasture in the middle of nowhere, nearly fifty miles outside Pecan Creek itself. It had taken Sheriff Moody, his deputies, and a handful of state troopers hours to locate the exact spot and recover the remains, even with Westmoreland riding shotgun. The child's clothing had been identified by his parents as what Kenny had been wearing the day he disappeared from his front yard.

The way everyone was talking around the squad room, Maggie knew they thought it was all over. That they'd as good as found Carrie Spencer's murderer as well.

The phones in the station had been lighting up like Fourth of July fireworks since the news leaked out, people calling to see if Litchfield was "safe" again, wanting to know if life could get "back to normal."

But Westmoreland still refused to confess to the kidnapping and killing of Carrie, and Maggie had a feeling he never would.

Ellen Spencer had phoned half a dozen times inquiring about Westmoreland's arrest, until Maggie had finally told her she'd head on over and answer all her questions face to face.

With the media swarming the station, wanting quotes from anyone who'd give them, Maggie was glad to escape.

She took her time heading across town, chewing over what she knew so far, squinting into the morning sunlight as she drove.

Ten minutes later, she pulled onto the Spencers' street, parking against the curb behind a Volvo. She glanced over at the Vincents' house as she shut her car door, catching the flutter of a curtain in the upstairs window.

Save for an woman in green warmups walking a golden retriever and a white-haired man out pruning his crepe myrtles, the sidewalks were quiet; the media vans that had clogged the street since Carrie's abduction were nowhere in sight. Probably because they'd moved camp to the Litchfield station, where they hovered around the desk sergeant, swarming any passing officer like killer bees.

She slung her handbag over her shoulder and headed up the pebbled walk to the front door.

It was Jake who answered her ring of the bell.

"Yeah?"

"Detective Ryan," she reminded him, as he stared at her blankly, like he'd never seen her before. His pupils were dilated, and she thought she smelled the vague cloying odor of pot smoke. "Is your mother home?"

His eyes widened, and he opened his mouth like he had something to say. Then his face closed up, and he withdrew into himself again. Without a word, he pushed the door wide open and headed off.

At least he hadn't called her "pig."

Maggie went in and stood inside the foyer, looking around her. "Mrs. Spencer?" she called out and waited as footsteps approached.

Tom Spencer rounded the corner.

He shook his head as he saw her, crossing his arms over his red cashmere sweater. "Why can't you leave us alone? Don't you think it's hard enough to lose a child without having to grieve in public?"

"Ellen phoned me."

"Oh, she did?"

"Yes."

"She's lying down," he said quickly, looking ready to usher her out. "And the rest of us are eating lunch. So if you've come to tell us about that kid Westmoreland, all we care about is that you've got him locked up."

He was giving her the brush-off, and Maggie wasn't in the mood. "If you'd just tell your wife that I'm here."

"Detective Ryan?" Ellen appeared on the stairs, clutching the banister. She wore a bathrobe, the sash loosely tied around her waist. "Thank you for coming so quickly."

Maggie nodded. "That's okay."

Tom intercepted his wife at the base of the steps. "What's this all about?" he asked as she descended, her slippers made soft slaps on the carpet. "Ellen, would you look at me when I'm talking to you?"

He caught her by the wrist, but Ellen pulled away, shoving her hands into the pink terry pockets.

"Let's go into the den, Detective, please."

"For God's sake," Tom uttered in protest, but Ellen had already started up the hallway.

Maggie went after her, and Tom followed on their heels.

She entered the dark-paneled den and settled down on the sofa. Ellen sat at its other end, her slippered feet curled beneath her.

Tom Spencer stayed apart from them, standing by the fireplace, looking as if he wanted nothing more than for it all to disappear.

"Did the man you've arrested...did he kill my daughter?" Ellen asked pointedly.

Her pale face was almost child-like framed as it was by her tangled hair, the look in her eyes so imploring that Maggie wasn't about to lead her on, though false promises would have been all too easy to make. "He hasn't confessed to it, no," she said, wishing her answer could be different. "It's still an ongoing investigation."

"But you think he did it?"

She might be the only one who didn't. "We're looking into it, of course."

"But he could be the one?" Tom Spencer asked. Maggie looked over at him, sizing him up, trying to find something there that would tell her what kind of man he really was, but seeing only a middle-aged male with still handsome features, graying hair and wrinkled brow.

"He could be the one," she said deliberately, picking

and choosing her words. "Right now, he's our prime suspect."

Tom Spencer nodded and walked away from the fireplace. He rounded the heavy writing desk and paused at the window to peer through the blinds. "We just want this to end," he said as if to himself. Then he dropped the blinds and turned around, fixing his gaze on his wife. "We just want it to be over so we can start picking up the pieces again."

Ellen shifted her eyes away from his, instead staring down at her lap.

"I'd like this case closed, too," Maggie said, "which is why I need you're help."

"Our help?" Tom echoed.

"If you could answer some questions..."

"Questions?" His cheeks flushed. "What the hell's going on? What else can we say that'll do any good at this point? You've got her killer in custody."

"What," Ellen quietly interrupted him, "is it you need from us?"

Tom sighed and faced the window.

"I'd like Dr. Spencer to tell me how he came in possession of Carrie's pink ribbon."

He swung around. His eyes squinted. "What in hell did you say?"

Maggie saw the horror in his face and felt her heart pound. The pink grosgrain strips were identical in every respect. She had checked it out herself. She forced her voice to stay steady, and said, this time more slowly, "Tell me about the pink ribbon your wife found in your bureau drawer. I want to know how you got it."

"Ellen?" he said, but she wouldn't look at him.

"If you came upon it innocently, why didn't you contact us about it?" Maggie asked, tired of how he always backed away from the truth, evading her questions by questioning her in turn.

"You think it was anything other than innocent? Do you really believe that I..." he stopped, staring at her. He shook his head. "No...no, it wasn't like that. It's not what you think. I found it. I picked it up when I went out looking for Carrie." He wet his lips, glancing at Ellen again, as if she'd somehow bail him out of this.

But she didn't.

Maggie leaned forward. "Where did you find it, Doctor?"

"Near the storm drain on the west side of the park."

"Why didn't you tell anyone?"

"I don't know."

Maggie wasn't about to let go. Maybe he'd gotten off the hook in Greenwich, but it wouldn't happen here. "Tell me where you were the afternoon that Carrie disappeared."

Ellen lifted her head.

"I was at Methodist."

"No, Dr. Spencer, you weren't," Maggie contested, noting how he avoided her stare. "Our officers spoke with the nursing staff, and they said you were gone before three. The ER paged you when one of your patients came in, and you'd disappeared."

"I was at my office."

"Your answering service phoned your private line several times, but no one answered."

"I didn't kill my own daughter."

185

"I wasn't accusing you."

"Aren't you?" he shouted at her, running his hand over his head. "Isn't that exactly what you're doing?"

Tom Spencer was doing a fine job of acting guilty without any help from her. Still, Maggie fought to keep cool. "You returned the hospital page from your car nearly an hour later. Your mobile phone company is working right now at pinpointing from where exactly the call was made."

"My God!" His cheeks flushed, he glared at her—furious. "You're the goddamned police, not the KGB!"

"Tom, please," Ellen whispered.

He turned away, but Maggie could see the twitch of his jaw, the strain of the tendons in his throat.

"I know why you left Connecticut," she went on, watching him squirm. "We've been in contact with the DA in Greenwich."

He kept his back to her.

"You've lied to us about where you were when your daughter was taken. You hid information from us about a piece of evidence." A carriage clock ticked on the mantle. Her pulse beat doubletime. "If you want us to find out who really killed Carrie, you have to be on our side, not against us."

"Shut up!" He raised his hands to his face, his shoulders shaking. "Shut up, goddammit! I didn't hurt my own child...I would never have hurt her."

Maggie heard Ellen's muffled sobs, and her mouth went dry. She had to dig to find her voice. "Where were you last Saturday afternoon between three and four o'clock?"

He shook his head. "I can't do this." He turned to his wife and whispered, "I'm so sorry, Ellen. I'm so sorry." Then he rushed from the room and was gone.

Maggie went out back to where a shed-like structure stood behind the garage of the house.

Tom's workshop.

Ellen had suggested it might be where he ran.

She knocked at the door, waiting for a moment before she pushed it open.

Sunlight slanted through grime-covered windows, dust dancing in its ghostly beams.

The floor beneath her feet was sprinkled here and there with sawdust. A chair with broken caning sat up-ended on a table. Above the workbench, Mason jars filled with nails and nuts and bolts stood side by side on the shelves like glass-bellied soldiers.

"Dr. Spencer?"

Somewhere outside, a bluejay squawked.

He obviously wasn't here.

She turned to leave, but curiosity got the best of her, and she found herself staying put.

She set down her purse and pulled open the workbench drawers, rifling through them, finding duct tape and rulers and hardware store whatnots. She checked inside the coffee cans stuck here and there, all of which held nails with varying degrees of rust.

A folded-up copy of *Playboy* had been shoved behind a red tool box, the pages dog-eared. Was this the good doctor's? she wondered. Or was it Jake's?

She stuck it back where she'd found it.

She reached above her head, drawing down an old cigar box, opening it up to find some rolling paper, a baggie filled with dried cannibus leaves, and several joints that were ready for business.

Again she found herself wondering, father's or son's?

"We found a handful of roaches."

"You found bugs?"

"Not cockroaches. Marijuana butts. Looks like someone used the place to smoke dope."

They'd recovered what was left of about half a dozen Marijuana cigarettes at the construction site where Carrie's body had been dumped. Maybe it was a longshot, but there were tests to compare papers, even the composition of the dried weed and traces of saliva.

Maggie lowered the lid, setting the box beside her purse.

There was a closed door just beyond the workbench, and she figured it was space used for storage.

She turned the knob and pushed. Hinges squealed, desperate for a shot of WD-40.

Beyond her nose, everything was black. A knotted string dangled overhead, and she gave it a tug. A bare bulb spat yellow light around her, illuminating a small room no bigger than a closet occupied by a countertop with plastic tubs, rows of chemicals, photographic paper, and a red-hued bulb above it all. A darkroom.

She hadn't realized Tom Spencer had time for a hobby.

A few photographs hung by laundry clips to a line strung from wall to wall. She took these down and looked them over.

A black-and-white shot of Ellen and Carrie in front of

the house. Another of Carrie alone, sitting on the hood of the BMW, her hair in pigtails, a smile on her face.

Maggie put them aside, tugging open a pair of drawers filled with more photographs, some of flowers, of clouds, and Carrie.

She picked up the wastebasket, a tall metal cylinder barely half full, and dumped its contents on the counter. Gingerly, she sifted through the pile, separating the empty bottles of chemicals, several underexposed and overexposed shots wadded into balls, and a strip of wrinkled negatives, which she pinched by its edges.

She held it up to the light, but the low wattage didn't provide enough contrast for her to make out much of anything.

She walked into the workshop, lifting the negatives to the glass of the window, holding them as flat as she could with the tips of her fingers, squinting at the succession of faces, of figures.

Jesus.

She closed her eyes and sighed.

Well, well, Dr. Spencer. Is this how you get your kicks?

She slipped the negatives carefully into her coat pocket, trying to still her trembling fingers.

She turned off the bulb in the darkroom and closed the door just as she'd found it. Then she picked up the cigar box and grabbed her purse, walking away from the workshop, cutting around the garage to the driveway and down to the street.

She was out of breath when she reached her parked car, and still breathing hard as she drove back to the station.

In less than an hour, the police photographer had printed up the negatives.

Maggie gathered up the photographs along with the envelope containing Carrie's "missing" ribbon and the bleak drawings Ellen had given her, taking everything to Sergeant Morris.

Forty-five minutes later, a car was dispatched to pick up Tom Spencer.

Maggie was ready for him.

Chapter Twenty

Maggie stared across the conference table at Tom Spencer and the gray-haired man in a slick-looking suit who sat beside him. She knew the lawyer by sight. Dick Landers. He was a high-priced Dallas defense attorney whose clientele was comprised of the rich and famous.

Tom Spencer must be scared for his life, she thought, calling in such a big gun before he'd say a word on the record.

Feeling guilty, Doc? She tipped her head, studying him, thinking his skin looked the color of putty. There wasn't much left of his arrogance now.

And with good reason.

She rubbed her hand over the manila envelope that lay before her on the table, the rolled-up drawings beside it.

Sarge sat on her right, and Phillips her left. Both had seen the evidence she'd presented and understood its implications. But no one was rushing into anything. The last thing the department needed was for news to get out that they'd dragged in Carrie Spencer's grieving daddy on suspicion of her murder.

"This is ridiculous," Dick Landers spoke up. He had one hand on Spencer's back. "I can't believe what's going on. Dr. Spencer just buried his little girl yesterday morning...."

"That's why he's here, Mr. Landers," Sarge cut him off. If he was feeling any pressure, he didn't show it. His bulldog's face was impassive as ever. "We're trying to find her killer."

Tom Spencer dropped his face into his hands. Landers absently patted his arm.

Maggie felt sick.

"Obstruction of justice? Tampering with evidence? Child pornography?" Landers scoffed, his pinched features pinkening. "Your threats are all nonsense! Dr. Spencer's an upstanding member of this community. Such accusations could very well ruin his career."

"We're after the truth is all, counselor," Sarge interjected, the edge in his voice clear. "Your client has interfered with a police investigation."

"My client has done nothing wrong."

"We'll see about that." Sarge turned to her and nodded. "Maggie?"

On cue, she unfastened the clasp on the manila envelope and withdrew a small sealed plastic bag. She handed it to Sarge, and he held it up.

Landers whispered something to Spencer, and the doctor looked up. His gaze fastened on the baggie.

"Do you recognize this, Dr. Spencer?" Sarge asked him. "It's a hair ribbon..."

"Obviously," Landers shot back.

"If you'd let me finish," Sergeant Morris countered, and

Landers shrugged.

Maggie noticed that Spencer had begun to sweat. His upper lip was slick with it. She tried to summon up some satisfaction at his discomfort, but felt only sadness and pity.

Sarge put the bag down on the table and poked it with his forefinger. "This is the twin to the pink ribbon that was found a few miles from where the body of Carrie Spencer was recovered. The girl's mother handed it over to Detective Ryan yesterday afternoon. She claimed it was in her husband's sock drawer."

"For Christ's sake!" Landers came up out of his chair and leaned over the conference table. He was flushed from his collar to the roots of his sparse hair. "This is outrageous!"

Maggie felt Phillips stir, heard him whisper something under his breath that she couldn't make out.

Sarge continued, undaunted, "When Detective Ryan questioned Dr. Spencer about the ribbon, he claimed to have picked it up near a storm drain on the west side of Litchfield Park."

Landers slid back into his seat. He bent over to Spencer, spoke into his ear, and the doctor nodded.

"That," Sarge went on, "is tampering with evidence, counselor. Even you should know that."

"My client's daughter had disappeared," the lawyer quickly countered. "He was in a state of shock...he was numb. He couldn't be expected to think clearly in such a situation."

"Dr. Spencer also lied to our detectives regarding his whereabouts between the hours of three and four p.m. last Saturday. Initially, he claimed to have been on-campus at Methodist Hospital, but those claims have proven false."

Again, Landers leaned toward Spencer and whispered. The doctor closed his eyes and hung his head.

Phillips nudged Maggie under the table. She tried to ignore him, but she felt it, too. Spencer had lied, and he'd gotten caught.

Finally, Landers straightened up. "No comment," he said, and Maggie knew then that he, too, had begun to understand the size of the holes in Spencer's story.

"Your client," Sarge said, "has hardly been a model citizen."

"Just cut to the chase, Sergeant, would you?"

Maggie slid the rubberband off Carrie's drawings, but Sarge caught her hand.

"The photographs," he said.

She set the drawings aside and reached for the envelope again, this time removing the prints made up from the negatives she'd found in Spencer's darkroom. There were half a dozen of them, all of children in various stages of undress and in unnatural poses, little better than amateur pornography.

She tried not to look at them herself as she fanned them out on the table, upside-down, so they faced Dr. Spencer.

She saw his eyes round, his jaw slackening as he took in the photos.

Thoughts swam through her head, of what Terry had said about the pictures drawn by Carrie, of the stick-figured man with the "penis," of the medical examiner's report of scarring in her anal tract, and she wondered if she was looking at a child molester. And killer.

"What the hell's going on? I don't know what you're trying to pull here," Landers barked, but Spencer set a hand on his arm, effectively shutting him up.

Tom Spencer reached across the table, drawing a photograph toward him with his fingertips.

It was a picture of Carrie.

"Where did you get this?" His eyes rose to Maggie. "Where?"

"They're yours, Dr. Spencer."

"No."

"I found them in your darkroom," she told him, her voice too high-pitched, her heartbeat too fast. "Your wife gave me permission." She caught herself, leaving it at that, knowing Ellen had not okayed her search of the premises, that the evidence likely would be dismissed in a court of law, but feeling justified at what she'd done nonetheless.

He took the photograph and held it, shaking his head. "No," he said again and again. "No...no...no." He crumpled it between his hands, pressing it into a ball.

Maggie glanced beside her at Sarge, but he was staring at Spencer with narrowed eyes.

"Do you often take pictures of children, Doctor?" he asked. "Is that your new hobby, or was it something you picked up while you were working in Connecticut? Seems you were a busy boy up in Greenwich. Three charges of professional misconduct. One involving a teenager. A mere child. You want to talk about it?"

Instantly Landers stepped in, "You don't have to say a word, Tom. Not a damned word." He turned on them, his cheeks flushed. "This is fucking outrageous!"

"No!" Spencer slapped his fists on the table, the crumbled photograph still grasped within the palm of his hand. "I didn't do it. I wouldn't hurt my daughter, I told you I'd never hurt her!"

"But the negatives were in your darkroom," Maggie said, anger pushing her half out of her chair. She gripped the arms to hold herself up, furious that he would try to deny what he'd done. "Explain that to me, Doctor?"

"I haven't used the damned darkroom in several months," he cried out with a shudder, ignoring the restraining hand Landers laid on his arm. "I didn't take them, don't you understand?"

"Then who did?"

"I don't know!"

Yes, you do, she wanted to shout at him, as Phillips reached for her and she settled back down. You know good and well who did. You see his face in your mirror every morning.

"Where were you on Saturday afternoon, Dr. Spencer," she persisted, feeling as close to breaking through his lies as she would ever get. She tried to stay cool, but she was too worked up. A tear of sweat slid down her back. "Were you near the park? Did you take Carrie?"

"My client doesn't have to answer..."

"I wasn't at the park," Spencer's voice cut him cold. "I didn't know Carrie was missing until I got home, I swear to God, I didn't."

His lawyer reached for him, but he pushed the hand away, shaking his head. The arrogant man from this morning was gone. In his place was someone who finally realized his life as he knew it was teetering on the brink, and his only chance to save any part of it was to stop hiding.

"All right, you win," he said softly. His fingers shook as

he laced them together atop the table. His eyes were downcast. "I'll tell you where I was, who I was with."

Phillips whispered, "The lying son of a bitch..."

Tom Spencer wet his lips, and, when he finally spoke, he sounded numb. "I was with someone. A woman. She's a nurse at the hospital. She has an apartment not two blocks from the park. I left Methodist just before three. I met her there." He paused, drawing in a breath. "I couldn't know that anything would happen to Carrie that day. I didn't think...."

No, you didn't think, Maggie wanted badly to tell him. Not with your head.

Never raising his head or opening his eyes he began to talk: "Her name is Jennifer...Jennifer Linden," he told them, and Phillips started writing in his notebook. "The Bayberry Apartments." His damp brow glistened beneath the fluorescent lamps. "She'll tell you I was with her...that I was there when the hospital paged me...when Ellen was looking for me, too." He closed his eyes. "I had my mobile phone in the apartment. That's where I called from"

When he opened his eyes, he looked at Maggie. "Though you probably know that already, Detective, don't you?"

She didn't respond to his egging. It was all she could do to remain quiet, to sit still.

He put his head in his hands, and his shoulders started shaking. "Oh, God, please, don't tell Ellen...please, you won't tell her, will you? After all she's been through...all I've put her through...." He broke down in noisy sobs.

Maggie watched him, feeling nauseous.

Sarge cleared his throat. "I'd like to speak with Dr.

Spencer and Mr. Landers alone."

Maggie pushed her chair away from the table and got up, her eyes on Spencer's shuddering back as she followed Phillips from the room.

He closed the door as she came out into the hallway, catching her by the shoulder.

"So where do we go from here?" he asked her, and Maggie found herself without an answer.

She'd been so sure about Tom Spencer.

Chapter Twenty-one

Maggie had something she needed to do, and told Phillips she'd be back in an hour.

She pushed out the security door and was passing the front desk, when she ran into Ellen Spencer.

"Where's Tom?" she asked, her thin hands grabbing at Maggie's coatsleeves. "Has he been arrested?"

"He's free to go, Mrs. Spencer," Maggie told her. "He and his lawyer are with Sergeant Morris, but they should be finished with him soon."

Jake strode up beside his mother, his hands jammed into his jeans pockets, hair nearly obscuring one eye altogether. The other glared at Maggie.

"If you'd like coffee, the machine's around the corner."

"Thank you." Ellen looked lonely and frightened, and Maggie pitied her again for what she would no doubt learn about the man she'd married.

With a sigh, she turned to leave.

A hand gripped her arm, and she was jerked around, coming face to face with Jake.

"My father's not the one you want, Detective," he hissed at her, his breath sour in her face. "My dad couldn't kill anyone."

"Jake, please," Ellen intervened, and the boy let go with a push. He shoved his hands in his pockets and walked away.

"I'm sorry," Ellen said, glancing at her son who sulked by the water fountain. "He's always been high strung, but these last few days..."

"It's okay." Maggie managed a smile, brushing at her sleeve. "It's a rough time for everyone."

Ellen nodded, and Maggie left her standing there, heading out the doors to the parking lot.

She knew her route by heart and drove without paying much attention to the passing street signs and houses.

She rolled her window down, letting the air blow at her, a hint of warmth despite the crispness. Winter didn't last much past February in Dallas, if even that. And then when summer came, it dragged on and on like an unwanted houseguest.

The sun glinted off her windshield, and she squinted against its brightness. She had never worn sunglasses. She just didn't like them.

"You can't hide from me, Magpie...you can't hide."

A shadow fell across her line of vision.

A face filled her mind.

The glisten of eyes, peering down at her, the smell of aftershave cutting off her breath, the dip of a mattress beneath her body.

A horn blared, and Maggie flinched. She'd veered

across the white line in the road's center, a Chevy pickup swerving to avoid her.

She pulled the wheel right, taking the car onto the shoulder, gravel kicking up under her wheels. Dust rose up like clouds around her as she parked, her heart thudding against her ribcage, ears ringing.

Fingers curled around the steering wheel, she leaned her forehead down against it, catching her breath, telling herself to calm down.

What the hell was wrong with her?

Why was it coming back now?

The nightmares, the fleeting memories that seemed all too real. The voice in her head that wouldn't remain where she had buried it.

She rubbed a hand over her eyes, knowing what had set her off.

The little girl.

She'd been a year older than Carrie when it had started. Daddy took off when she was five, leaving her behind, tearing her world apart as she knew it, stealing away her feelings of comfort and safety. Momma had told her it was all her fault, and Maggie had believed her. Six months after, Momma'd found another man and remarried. They'd moved to Mockingbird, to the little white house. Momma told her he'd take Daddy's place and make them happy, but it wasn't true.

She raised her head, wiping her sleeve across her face, catching sight of her eyes in the rearview mirror.

He's dead, Maggie, she reminded herself. He's been dead for seventeen years. He can't hurt you anymore.

"He made us a family again... she heard her Momma's

voice, and shook her head. No, that's not how it was. It had gone on for eight years, and Momma had never made him stop. How could she not have known?

She shivered, teeth chattering. She was losing it, losing control.

Get a grip, she told herself, fighting her panic, feeling her pulse ebb, her heartbeat slow down.

She blinked against the sun, and reached up for the visor, angling it to shade her eyes from the light.

Then she started up the car and guided it off the shoulder and into the right lane, passing open fields where horses and cows grazed, where discarded Big Gulps and wrappers from Big Macs littered the line of fence.

Within another mile, half-built houses sprang up beyond signs touting, "Litchfield Estates—Homes from $350,000," and flags that flapped about in the wind above a trailer which was no doubt the builder's on-site office.

Barely two miles beyond was Litchfield Park.

She slowed the car as she approached. A young mother pushed her child on the swingset, tiny legs kicking the air. A pair of ladies in pastel sweatsuits strolled across the grass. Several boys climbed on the jungle gym. An older man walked a terrier.

The sky above them was blue and clear. Birds chirruped from the trees. Every now and then, through her opened window, Maggie heard laughter.

As if nothing had happened, she thought. As if a little girl had never died. As if the world were a safe place after all.

She drove on ahead, weaving through the adjacent neighborhoods with their two and three-story brick houses, and curved driveways with shiny foreign cars.

She turned onto Sparrow, picking her way up the street. A dirtbike with a helmeted rider came at her from the other direction, speeding past so quickly that she saw only the back of a leather jacket in her rearview mirror.

She pulled up to the curb in front of the Vincent's and shut off the engine, taking her time to gather up her purse and the manila envelope, collecting her thoughts, before she got out and walked up the driveway toward the door.

Barbara answered the bell.

"Detective? Is something wrong?"

"Do you have a minute?" she asked. Barbara Vincent nodded, inviting her in.

She led Maggie from the marble-tiled foyer and into the den where Maggie had spoken with Tyler the day before. She settled down on the sofa and gestured for Maggie to join her.

The house was quiet.

"You just missed Tyler," Barb said as if reading her thoughts. "He took off on that damned motorbike of his."

"So that's who nearly ran me over."

Barb made a face, resting an arm atop a cushion, silver bracelets gently clinking. "I know, he goes too fast, doesn't he? So many kids have 'em. All driving around like lunatics. Lord, but I dread the day that boy'll get his driver's license."

Maggie smiled. "And where's Ashley?"

Barbara glanced back toward the foyer. "She's upstairs napping. She hasn't been sleeping real well at night since Carrie was found."

Maggie remembered how Ashley had clung to the banister, crying for her mother, and Tyler looking embarrassed as he'd chased her up the stairs.

"Could I help you with something?" Barbara prompted.

Maggie opened up the envelope in her lap and slid out photographs made from the negatives she'd found in Tom Spencer's darkroom, only these were just headshots, cropped off at the neck.

She handed all but the one of Carrie over to Barbara.

"What's this about?"

"Do you know these children?" Maggie asked. "It's important that we get their names."

Barb looked puzzled, but turned her attention to the photographs, going through them one by one. When she had seen them all, she glanced up. "I recognize most of them, yes."

"Do they live in the neighborhood then?"

"The ones I know do."

"Would you identify them for me, Mrs. Vincent?"

Barb took the topmost picture and set it down on the cushion between them. "This is Katie Anderson. Her mama's on the PTA at the elementary school." She lay the second atop it. "This one's Tiffany Reed. She took day care with Ashley." Then more tentatively. "I think this one's Timmy Martin, and this other Bethany Kane." There were only two she didn't know.

Maggie had her go over the names again, this time writing them down on the backs of the photographs. She also recorded any addresses that Barbara was familiar with.

When she left ten minutes after, she had the pictures carefully tucked into her purse.

As she drove back to the station, she ran through the names, over and over.

The more she reviewed them, the more familiar they sounded, as if she'd seen them before, though she couldn't think why or when.

When she got back to the station, Phillips was waiting for her.

"Tom Spencer volunteered to take a polygraph," he told her, looking as if he hardly believed it himself. "He also gave us a set of his prints for comparison."

The lab had removed several partials from the negatives, and Maggie held her breath as he finished, "They're not his. There's no match."

"And the polygraph?"

"He passed with flying colors."

She tugged off her coat and dumped it over the back of her chair. Then she pulled her notebook from her purse, setting it in front of her. She opened up the file on Carrie Spencer, drawing out the reports on Kenny Wayne and his accused killer, Brian Westmoreland.

Propping her chin on her fist, she started to read, line by line, page by page. Once, and then twice over.

The facts were pitifully few.

Carrie Spencer had disappeared from Litchfield Park sometime late last Saturday afternoon. No one had seen anything, nor had a child's cries been heard.

A search the next morning had turned up a ribbon and a shoe, both identified as Carrie's, the sneaker with a blood stain that proved to be O positive.

The girl's body was found by a construction worker

sometime after dawn on Monday morning, less than forty-eight hours after she'd vanished. The body had been moved, the crime scene disturbed.

Maggie leaned back in her chair. They didn't have much to go on. They hadn't from the start.

Brian Westmoreland had seemed the perfect suspect. He was a known child molester, and he was there at the park. He was O positive, matching the stain on the sneaker, but the DNA tests were still out, and there were too many Type O's around Litchfield to convict him on that alone.

Still, Maggie wasn't sure he was their man. He had confessed to killing the boy from Pecan Creek, but he swore he hadn't taken Carrie, and Maggie believed him.

He had no reason to lie about Carrie and, besides, the MO in her case varied on several points.

The boy had been dumped in a ditch off a farm road in Pecan County.

Carrie had been taken to a half-built house not more than two miles from Litchfield Park. A site littered with the remnants of somebody's joints.

Maggie had a feeling that the particular place was known to whoever took Carrie, that she was brought there for a reason. He could've been well aware that the construction crews only worked half-days on Saturday, that it was isolated from prying ears and eyes.

Had he picked Carrie because he knew her? Because she felt safe with him? Or maybe the opposite. He could have scared her into going.

Maggie suddenly realized she was grinding her teeth. She tried to relax, drawing in a deep breath.

Tom Spencer had an alibi for Saturday afternoon, one that had checked out. Jennifer Linden had backed up his story and was coming in sometime this evening to sign an affidavit.

"My father's not the one you want...my dad couldn't kill anyone..."

Jake's words rang in her head. She saw his flushed face again, heard the conviction in his voice.

He sounded so sure.

Or was he just standing up for his father?

"...not the one you want..."

Was he protecting someone? Did he know something he wasn't telling? Why did he seem so afraid? For his father? Or for himself?

Westmoreland. Spencer. Jake.

Christ, why did she feel like she was running around in circles?

She reached for the list of names she'd gotten from Barbara Vincent, going over addresses as well, checking them with a map to see how near they all lived to each other, wondering who would have had access to each child, enough time alone to undress them and pose them without someone else walking in?

Katie Anderson.

Tiffany Reed.

Timmy Martin.

Bethany Kane.

She pressed her eyes closed and repeated the names.

Where had she seen them before?

Why were they so familiar?

Anderson, Reed, Martin, Kane.

She stopped, and her eyes came open.

"Jesus," she whispered.

She rummaged through the papers on her desk, looking for another file. Snatching it up, she rifled through it, finally finding what she sought.

Her mouth went dry.

There they were.

Anderson, Reed, Martin, and Kane, all present among the families listed as victims in the pet killing case.

Her head began to pound with the noise of her heart.

Had someone targeted these children? To scare them so they wouldn't tattle? So that they'd pose for photographs and allow themselves to be abused?

Were the pictures not enough anymore? Was it too little just to touch them? Was the time too fleeting? Did he want more excitement, something rougher and more thrilling?

"...everyone thought it was Jake..."

Barbara Vincent had been sure he'd been behind the animal killings.

Maggie found herself wondering if he had killed Carrie, too.

Chapter Twenty-two

"There's something you're not telling me," Phillips said as he drove. The light slipped from yellow to red in front of them, and he slowed to a stop. The vinyl seat crackled as he shifted his weight, turning his head. "You want to let me in on it, Ryan?"

Maggie felt self-conscious under his scrutiny and avoided his eyes. Beneath the orange glow of the streetlamps, a brisk parade of sedans and compact cars crossed the intersection, their colors dimmed by the coming night and by the grime leftover by winter.

"Maggie?"

"It's green," she said, pointing up at the signal.

Phillips grunted, facing front again, pulling through the light.

Her head pounded with uncertainties, forgotten snatches of conversation, impressions and images, and those gut instincts Phillips had always told her to trust.

"You think Jake knows something, don't you?" Phillips asked.

"I think he's scared shitless," she said, having seen it in his face at the station earlier. Despite his tough guy act, he was just a kid. Whatever secret he was holding onto was getting to him.

"Scared enough to confess?"

"I don't know. Maybe, yes."

In another five minutes, they turned onto Woodlawn then Sparrow. The streetlights shed dull orange onto the sidewalk every half-block. Porch lamps and spots flooded yards with almost day-like brilliance. Maggie wondered how many children were sleeping with the lights on inside as well.

You could buy state-of-the-art alarm systems and fancy deadbolts, and still you couldn't be sure your children were safe. Especially if you were locking in whatever they feared the most.

The brakes squeaked as Phillips bumped the car against the curb to park.

Maggie didn't wait for him to cut the ignition before she climbed out.

The slap of the car door punctuated the stillness. No one was in sight. The air was edged with cold, and she drew in a deep breath, slipping her purse over her shoulder as she cut across the lawn toward the house.

Phillips came up behind her as she rang the bell.

A moment later, Ellen opened the door.

She looked at them without speaking, and Maggie suddenly felt like an intruder, one who had invaded this woman's privacy far too often—who wasn't welcome anymore. Her face bore Ellen's devastation in the hard lines between nose and mouth, the blotchy tone of her skin, and eyes swollen from too many tears and too little sleep.

"Tom isn't here," she finally spoke, her voice soft, slightly slurred. "He's moved out. I need some time alone to think."

"I'm sorry." Maggie glanced at Phillips. "But we didn't come to see your husband. We're here to see Jake."

If Ellen was surprised, she didn't show it. She simply nodded and drew the door fully open, holding onto it.

She stepped ahead of Phillips into the foyer. A television set was turned on somewhere. The familiar buzz of canned laughter reached her ears.

"Follow me," Ellen said and walked away, her slippered feet shuffling on the carpet as she disappeared up the hallway.

Phillips shrugged, and Maggie started on after her, hearing Ellen's raised voice up ahead in the den.

Maggie picked up her steps, feeling a rush of cold as she entered the room to find Ellen standing alone in its midst, the TV still on.

The sliding glass door was wide open.

"Shit."

She shoved her purse into Phillips' arms and took off running.

She rushed out onto the patio, spotting Jake slipping through the rear gate.

Maggie darted after him.

She emerged into the alley. Darkness obscured her vision.

Her loafers slapped hard on the pavement, and she

pumped her arms as she raced after the shadow that was Jake, the tattoo of his footsteps as clear as her own.

The pant of her breath came louder, filling her head.

She ran past closed garages, high-board fences, over uneven ground.

And he slipped farther away.

Her blood rushed with her frantic pace.

"Jake!" she got out. "Jake!"

She was losing him. He was already at the mouth of the alley, more than half a block ahead.

"Jake!"

Sudden headlights filled her eyes, sweeping around the corner, into the alleyway.

Jake was silhouetted in their beams.

With a horrifying thud, the car hit him.

His body bounced across the hood, then was tossed aside into the pitch, beyond the glare of the headlamps.

Brakes squealed.

The car stopped.

"Jake!"

Maggie sprinted ahead despite a stitch in her side, fighting down her panic, eyes blinded by the high beams.

The driver appeared, black against the glare. "I didn't see him," he shouted. "I didn't see him."

She found Jake on the car's other side, lying on his back on the concrete.

Blood trickled from his nose and mouth.

His eyes were closed. His right leg was twisted beneath him. Jesus, she thought. Jesus.

She tried to catch her breath as she knelt beside him,

feeling for a pulse at his wrist then at his neck, finding shallow movement.

"Is he all right?" The driver leaned over her shoulder, casting shadow on Jake's face. "I've got a car phone..."

Maggie yelled up at him, "Call 911...get an ambulance here...Christ!"

She couldn't move him. There could be head injuries, internal bleeding.

He moaned, and her heart leapt.

"Jake?" she bent closer, stroking his hair with her fingers, brushing it from his face. "Jake?"

His eyelashes fluttered. "Mom?" he whispered, a child's voice, small and frightened. "Mommy?"

Maggie held his hand, firmly clasping it between her own. It was cold and clammy. "Hush," she soothed him, "Try not to move. The ambulance is on its way."

His skin was so pale. The blood looked black against it.

"It's okay," she said, "it's okay," over and over again, holding onto him until the wail of sirens and flashing lights filled the alley.

Chapter Twenty-three

Maggie waited at Methodist Hospital until well past midnight when they finally finished surgery to relieve pressure on Jake's brain and to set pins in his right leg. She saw Ellen from across the room, but when she tried to approach her, she was waved away.

When Maggie left, Jake was sleeping a drug-induced sleep in ICU. If she was lucky—if he was lucky—she could possibly talk to him in the morning.

Phillips took her back to the station to pick up her car. Then she drove home.

As soon as she walked through the door, a wave of exhaustion washed over her. She was too tired to eat. She felt dirty, tainted by what she'd seen, by what she thought she knew.

She peeled off her clothes and got into the shower, the water turned as hot as she could stand it.

She closed her eyes as the spray pounded her skin, seeing flashes of Jake running away, hearing the thump as the car hit him, playing each through her mind again and again.

In spite of the steam, she was shivering.

She shut off the shower and toweled herself dry, rubbing at her hair until the curls were barely damp. She donned flannel pajamas and heavy socks, and still her teeth chattered.

She went to bed, curling up beneath the covers, pulling the comforter under her chin.

Jake was terrified of something. Or someone. And she had a feeling he'd been afraid for a long while, long enough so that he didn't know how to free himself from it.

She stared at the clock, watching the green numbers change every minute.

Who was it Jake feared so much?

Sighing, she turned on her side, then flopped onto her back.

What was she missing?

She thought of what Barbara Vincent had once told her, about Ellen never leaving Carrie alone with her brother, of Tyler telling her that Jake wasn't as bad as everyone believed. Closing her eyes, she remembered Ashley Vincent's tear-stained face, the haunting photographs framed in silver on the family's coffee table.

What didn't she see?

She pushed a fist against the pillow, pressing her face to its softness.

She was so tired.

Fog seeped through her mind, and she fell asleep.

"Magpie? Magpie, it's me."

She heard the voice and feigned sleep. She always hoped he would see her eyes were closed and let her alone. But it never worked.

He was humming very softly. He never wanted to wake Momma. "It's our secret," he would tell her. "Just between you and me."

She held her breath, thinking she could make herself invisible, that if she pretended she was somewhere else, she would be.

But the door clicked shut, and she listened to the shuffle of his feet.

No, she repeated in her mind like a prayer. No, no, no.

Then the mattress dipped, and she felt his hand come down atop the covers, resting on her hip.

She tried to lay still, forced her eyes to stay shut, hoping he would leave her alone this time, that he would understand she didn't want him. That when he did this to her, she felt dirty and sick.

His fingers caught themselves in her hair, tugging hard so that she gasped, and he laughed, knowing she was awake.

"It won't take long, I promise, sweet."

His hand slid down her cheek to her throat, before he peeled back the blanket, and she drew her legs up to her chest, holding on tightly, bending her head so that her brow touched her knees. "Please," she whispered, "please."

Which only made him laugh again, as if something she'd said had amused him.

He leaned nearer. She could smell his breath, foul with the whiskey he rarely drank in front of Momma, but always before his nightly visits. "Come on, Magpie. Be a good girl for me."

And then he pulled her arms to her sides, moving her legs flat on the bed, all the while she whimpered, tears sliding over her cheeks.

He hummed as he drew up her nightgown and dug his fingers beneath the elastic of her panties, pushing them down.

She closed her eyes, biting down on her lip till she tasted blood, afraid to cry, afraid to call out, knowing he would make it worse if she did and it hurt enough as it was.

His weight fell upon her, and she gasped for air. She couldn't breathe...oh, God, she couldn't breathe....

Maggie bolted upright, hyperventilating, tears streaming down her cheeks.

She pushed her hands flat on the bed, her shoulders rocking as she tried to breathe. Just breathe.

"Momma," she whispered, "help me."

She reached her arms around her knees, her body trembling, her skin prickled with gooseflesh.

It wouldn't go away. No matter how she fought, it wouldn't disappear.

Through the darkness, she stared at the telephone on the nightstand. She reached out, her fingers touching the plastic, picking up the receiver, only to drop it down again.

The clock showed four-fifteen.

Terry would be sleeping. And Maggie didn't want to wake her.

She forced herself to calm down, and her heartbeat slowed. But she knew she wouldn't sleep.

She pushed back the covers and swung her legs around,

dropping her feet to the floor. Flannel stuck to her skin. Her hair was wet with perspiration.

She went into the bathroom and showered again, getting in and out quickly. She dried her hair which fell as it always did in brown waves around her face. She pulled on a pair of jeans and a turtleneck.

She drank a glass of orange juice before she donned her coat and left. She drove to the hospital in the dark of early morning, the sky navy and scattered with stars, the crescent moon still hanging.

The rattle of heat through the vents and the hushed thump of tires on the street worked to soothe her rattled nerves, and when she reached the hospital, she felt more in control.

She followed the path she'd taken the night before, guided by arrows and overhead signs. Fluorescent lights cast a yellow-green pallor over everything, and did nothing to erase the fatigue from the faces of the nurses in ICU.

Jake's surgeon wouldn't make his rounds until seven, so Maggie got herself a cup of coffee from the vending machine and settled into one of the dozen waiting-room chairs. Propping her feet atop a coffee table scattered with dog-eared magazines, she lay back her head, intending to close her eyes just for a moment.

"Detective Ryan?"

A hand shook her shoulder, and Maggie came awake, blinking sleep from her eyes. She put her feet on the floor and checked her watch. The hands showed seven-fifteen.

"I didn't mean to disturb you."

"No, it's all right. I'm glad you did."

She stood, smoothing a hand over her coat, picking up

her purse.

Jake's surgeon folded his down-covered arms over his green scrubs. Gold wire-rimmed glasses perched on the bridge of his nose, his dark eyes magnified behind them. "His vital signs are stable. He's doing remarkably well considering what he's been through. He's awake, if you'd like to see him."

"I would."

"I can give you five minutes, but no more."

"I'll take it."

She followed him through a pair of doors and around a corner. He caught her arm before he left her. "Five minutes," he reminded, before he was gone.

She saw Jake through the window of the nurses' station. A ponytailed woman in scrubs glanced up from checking his IV. She moved from monitor to monitor, scribbling onto a chart which she carried with her when she brushed past Maggie and headed out.

For a minute, Maggie stood in the doorway, just looking at him. His right leg was up in traction, a white sheet draped across him like a tent. Gauze wrapped his head, and she could tell they'd shaved off the long hair that usually hid half his face. His nose was bruised, the skin below his eyes purpled.

She went nearer, coming up beside him. She rested her hands on the metal guardrail.

"Jake?"

She thought he was asleep, until she caught the movement of his hand, the wrist wrapped with a plastic ID. His dark lashes fluttered, and his eyes opened to slits.

She leaned over. "Can you hear me?"

He croaked softly, "Yes."

She folded her arms on the rail, hearing the rhythmic blips of his pulse on the monitor. "Won't you tell me," she whispered, "what it is you're afraid of? Because I don't think it was me you were running from last night."

He didn't answer. He just lay there very still, but the bleeps on the monitor quickened.

She knew he was listening.

"I think I finally understand what was going on," she told him, hoping to God she was on the right track, the idea only having come to her last night. "I think I know who killed those animals in your neighborhood and why he did it. He probably was relieved when they thought it was you, right? When he knew all along what the truth was. When you knew."

His lashes glistened, the tears pooling in the murky bruises beneath his eyes. But he said nothing.

"You let him use your father's darkroom to develop the pictures he took of the children. Maybe you even helped him." Maggie bent nearer, breathing in the smell of antiseptics, of starched sheets and plastic tubes. "Did it scare you, being part of his secret? Or did it make you feel like a big man? Like you were breaking the rules."

He turned his head away ever so slightly, and she reached down, touching his cheek with the back of her hand.

"C'mon, Jake. You can't let him get away with it. He's sick. He needs help, not protection. You know that, don't you? You were frightened enough of what he might do to watch out for your sister, staying home whenever your parents left him alone with her."

"No," he said, the word a moan, "it was an accident."

"An accident?" She drew back her hand.

His eyes cracked open, the whites of them red-veined. "I was there...at the house...rode my bike." He paused to wet dry lips, and Maggie took his hand, squeezing it to urge him on. "It was too late...she was already dead...he said he didn't mean to...that it was a mistake...he needed to hide her...I freaked out...I was high...I didn't think...I couldn't think." He slipped his hand from her fingers and raised it to his face. He was crying now, shaking.

Maggie's heart raced.

"He had a camera...he took her picture," Jake murmured, and the monitor above him began to beep a ragged beat. "He said he wanted a souvenir."

Her picture.

Maggie stood up straight.

Sweet Jesus.

"I'm sorry, but you'll have to go."

A nurse in green scrubs came up beside her, and Maggie nodded, backing away.

At the door, she hesitated, watching as the woman flipped down Jake's bedrail, bending over him; all the while above them the machine blipped incessantly.

She went to the nurses' station and borrowed the phone, calling John Phillips, telling him what she knew and where she was headed.

"I'll meet you there," she said when she was finished.

Then she hung up and left.

Chapter Twenty-four

Tyler Vincent had murdered Carrie.

The thought rang through her head as she maneuvered her car through the streets, driving faster than she should.

She blinked against the glare the sun cast on her windshield, remembering the black-and-white pictures she'd seen in the Vincents' living room. She would bet her badge Tyler had been the one behind the camera.

And she had no doubt that his fingerprints would match up with the partials the lab had recovered on the negatives she'd found in Tom Spencer's wastebasket.

Litchfield Park rose up before her, and, by habit, she slowed as she passed.

She thought of the helmeted figure on the motorbike that had sped past her before. "So many kids have 'em these days," Barbara Vincent had said, and Maggie realized she was right. No one would have taken note of a teenager on a dirtbike cruising the park on Saturday. With his helmet on, Tyler would have been anonymous, looking much like any of the other rich Litchfield kids with their expensive toys. No one would've seen his face. No one would have paid him the slightest attention.

The motorbike.

If he hadn't wiped it off, Carrie's prints might be on it, perhaps even her hairs or fibers from her clothing.

Maggie hit her palm against the steering wheel, wondering how she could've been so wrong this time. She'd sensed early on that it wasn't a stranger abduction, that someone on the inside had killed Carrie. Her training had taught her that everyone's a suspect, but she hadn't seriously believed that the well-behaved 15-year-old boy she'd spoken with in the days before could have murdered Carrie.

She had been so sure it was the girl's father.

And she knew why. She'd let her own past affect her judgment. Her emotions had ruled her brain, and she'd let herself get sidetracked because of it.

The child inside herself had figured to right the wrongs done long ago. To punish the father.

She had wanted it to be him.

She pushed her foot down on the gas, heading up Woodlawn and turning on Sparrow.

She pulled the car against the curb in front of the Vincents'.

She stared up at the facade of brick with its wood shingled roof and brass light fixtures, and she wondered what if anything had gone on behind its walls to make a young boy grow up to kill?

The curtains parted in an upstairs window, but as quickly, they dropped again.

She unzipped her leather bag and reached inside, fingers touching her holstered .38, then she withdrew her hand and slipped her purse over her shoulder.

Steeling herself, she walked up to the door and rang the bell.

"Detective Ryan?"

Barb stood in the jamb dressed in navy pants with a pale pink cashmere sweater, her hair neatly brushed, her make-up perfect.

Ashley toddled up behind her, peering at Maggie from around her mother's thigh. Barbara's hand reached down to rest on her daughter's head.

"Is there something I can do for you?" she said, looking both confused and impatient. "I've got to finish feeding Ash, then drive her over to preschool. Frank's already gone, and Tyler's upstairs getting dressed."

"Could you have him come down, please."

Ashley was fidgeting, grabbing at her mother's sweater. "He has to be at school in half an hour. If you could come back this afternoon..."

"This can't wait, Mrs. Vincent."

"Is it about Jake?" She clicked tongue against teeth. "We heard what happened last night."

"Is Tyler upstairs?" Maggie asked, anxious to get on with this.

Ashley tugged at her mother's pants, and Barbara sighed, catching hold of the girl's hand, nodding at Maggie. "Third door on the right. Go on ahead. I'll come on up after I've gotten Ash fed."

Barbara herded the girl away, and Maggie headed for the steps, taking them up two at a time.

The third door on the right was shut, so she knocked lightly before she tried the knob, half-expecting it was locked.

It turned in her hand, and she pushed the door open. "Tyler?"

"Detective, hi."

He was sitting on his bed, his back against a pair of pillows, his knees drawn up, the rumpled comforter beneath him. She glanced over to the window and realized it was his curtains she'd seen stir when she'd arrived.

Had he known she was coming?

"Would you shut the door," he said, his voice quiet.

Maggie figured he knew why she was here and wanted some privacy from his mother.

"Please."

"All right," she said, pushing it closed with a click.

"Thank you," he said and hugged his knees.

His pale brown hair was still damp from the shower. He had good features, ones that promised he'd be handsome some day. He had clear skin and clear eyes, a soft mouth.

It would be easy to forget what he had done. Easier not to believe it.

"I heard about Jake," he said. "Is he okay?"

"He'll be all right." She took a step further in, looking around her, at shelves filled with books and model airplanes. A chair strewn with clothes. A computer with monitor and laser printer. An entertainment center held a television set and stereo system better than any she could afford.

"I just left the hospital," she said, going slowly. "I had

the chance to talk with Jake." She turned to face him. "About you."

Tyler said nothing. Something flickered in his eyes, but his calm expression did not alter. He didn't seem surprised by her statement.

Maggie kept an arm's length between herself and the bed. She didn't take her eyes off him. "Jake told me what he saw last Saturday afternoon. He said he rode his bike to the construction site and found you there with Carrie. He said she was already dead, and he helped you hide her in the dumpster."

"He lied." Tyler shook his head. "He's so crazy...you can't really believe him." He screwed up his face. "Jake's a pothead, you know. He gets high and makes things up."

He was so convincing, she would have believed him if she hadn't known better. "We found a strip of negatives in the trash in Dr. Spencer's darkroom. Pornographic pictures of children. They're yours, aren't they?" He frowned, but otherwise he didn't answer. "All we have to do is match your fingerprints..."

"They're Jake's, I'll bet. Why don't you print him and see if they're his? He used his father's darkroom all the time. He's the one who showed me how to develop film."

But Maggie wasn't buying his lies. This time, Jake wouldn't take the fall. She wouldn't let him.

"We'll know soon enough. My partner's getting a warrant to search the house and your room," she said, amazed at his self-control, wondering how he could stay so cool, so still, when everything was caving in around him. "Forensics'll go over your dirtbike with tweezers, and I'll bet they come up with Carrie's prints, fibers from her clothes, maybe some of her hair. Enough to incriminate you, Tyler."

He stared at her, unblinking. As if his mind were on something else entirely.

"I've already spoken with the parents of the children in the pictures. They've confirmed you've been babysitting. They also admit they had pets killed awhile back. Though I think you know that, too."

She fell silent, having expected something else from him. Shouted denials. Hysterics. Tears. Rage.

Anything but silence.

She turned away from him, trying to get herself together, to keep herself in check.

It was then she saw his camera.

She went over to his bureau and crouched down to look at it. An expensive Nikon with a telephoto lens and all sorts of buttons that did God knows what. She leaned toward the "idiot proof" models and still her photographs were usually overexposed and off-center.

She drew it toward her with the tip of her finger, checking the number of exposures left, talking as she did to fill up the minutes. "You never even mentioned that you liked photography, though I should've figured you had something to do with those pictures in your den. They're almost all of Ashley and your parents." She stared at the camera. "Jake told me you took Carrie's picture the day of the murder. Was she already dead? Or was it before you hit her with the brick..."

"You're wrong," he cut her off, his voice rising a bit. "Whatever Jake said, he's lying like he always does just to save his own skin."

"I believe him."

"You don't know anything...you don't understand any of it!"

Maggie lifted her eyes to the mirror just as she heard the click.

She caught his image in the glass and cursed under her breath. She turned around slowly to find that the mirror had not deceived her.

He was on his knees on the bed, a shotgun in his hands. He must have had it all along, hidden beneath the blankets.

She shook her head.

If there's one thing she didn't like about Texas, this was it. Daddies giving their small boys guns like they were toy trains. "Here, son, your very own 12-gauge Browning. Merry Christmas. Don't shoot the cat."

"Tyler, put that down, for Christ's sake."

He didn't even flinch. His eyes above the barrel stared her down. He was dead earnest.

Her hand reached for her purse, her fingertips encountering the zipper. Her .38 was inside, out of reach. She'd never needed it the entire two years she'd been on the Litchfield PD.

Until now.

"Don't," Tyler said, the slightest breathlessness in his voice. "Don't try anything."

Maggie lifted up her hands to pacify him, her gaze flitting around her, at the window with the drawn drapes, at the closed door, and she mentally berated herself for getting trapped like a goddamned squirrel.

Where was Phillips anyhow?

He should be here any moment.

Just keep him talking, Maggie, she told herself. Keep

him occupied.

She looked at Tyler.

He had not lowered the shotgun an inch.

"You murdered her, didn't you?" she asked him, forcing herself to show a calm she did not feel. "Jake was telling the truth. He'd been keeping your secrets."

The shotgun quivered.

"You molested her like the others, but you didn't kill them, Tyler." Her mouth was cotton, her voice a croak. "Why Carrie?"

He peered at her from above the gun's sight, and, for the first time, she saw fear in his eyes. "You don't understand."

"Try me."

Maggie heard her own breathing in the silence, her own heart pound.

"Why don't you tell me about it?"

The tip of his tongue came out to wet his lips. "You don't know what it feels like when someone makes you do things, when he hurts you, and you can't tell anyone because no one will believe you." His voice was flat. The total lack of emotion sent a chill up her spine. "He made me feel helpless...he didn't listen to me, he just did it. And nobody knew. No one listened. I didn't exist."

Bile rose in Maggie's throat.

"When I did it to them, I felt like I was somebody, that I was in control." A light went on in his eyes. "I could touch them, and they were mine for as long as I wanted, like they were pictures in a magazine, only real. They were afraid of me. They did whatever I said." He stopped suddenly, then he whispered, "Just like I did with him."

"Who was it, Tyler? Who hurt you so badly?"

The shotgun trembled in his hands. "I fucking loved him. I loved him."

"Who?" she said again, feeling sick.

"Grandad," he whispered. "I'd always thought he was like Santa Claus. He made me laugh...he brought me presents." He flushed and fury filled his voice. "Until he did what he did."

Maggie drew in a deep breath. Her knees felt shaky. She wanted to think he was making it up, that he was making excuses. But she knew it was true.

She knew.

"He took me on a fishing trip when I was seven...he told me it'd make me a man, and it didn't stop till he was dead."

Maggie saw them in her mind's eye, a little boy and an old man, and, despite everything, she felt empathy for him, with his impotence, his helplessness. She knew what it was to live in the fear of never knowing when it would start, when it would end.

"She was off by herself, playing near the storm drain on the side of the road, where nobody could see her. She said she'd seen a kitty-cat run down there and thought the ground had swallowed it up."

It took a second for Maggie to realize what he was talking about. That he was now telling her about Carrie.

"I drove around a couple times before I pulled up behind the parked cars. No one even noticed." He looked off, seeing something Maggie couldn't. "She picked up some glass and cut her finger. She started whimpering when she saw blood."

The barrel of the shotgun dropped slightly, but then he

seemed to realize what he'd done, and his face turned hard again, the barrel tipping up.

"I told her I'd take her to her father at the hospital, that he'd fix it, and she trusted me. She climbed onto the bike, and we took off. I held her as I drove, but she kept squirming. I had to carry her into the house...I was afraid she'd try to run. I never knew she'd lost a shoe. I was too pumped up, you know? Too wired."

He pressed his mouth in a tight line, his face pinched. "If she hadn't started screaming, it wouldn't have happened, none of it. I tried to make her stop, but she kept fussing. If she'd only kept quiet like I told her, I'd never have hit her...she wouldn't be dead if she'd listened...it's all her fault, you see?" He was shouting, his eyes bright, his skin flushed. "If she would've shut up...I wouldn't have needed....I had to kill her to make her stop screaming!"

The door flew open, and Barbara Vincent stood staring at Tyler.

"Dear God..."

In one swift movement, he swung the shotgun around and pulled the trigger.

Chapter Twenty-five

Maggie stood against the wall in the foyer as the morgue attendants brought the stretcher down the curving stairs, then guided it to the front door, disappearing through it. Behind them, a uniformed officer carried out something wrapped in a plastic trash bag.

The shotgun, she realized.

She stared, even after they were gone.

Her senses were numbed, dulled by what she'd seen. It didn't matter that she'd witnessed death in some form or another a dozen times before, that she'd smelled it and touched it.

It still horrified her.

The only way she could keep herself together was to shut everything out. To feel nothing rather than the flood of emotions that would surely drown her.

She could hear crying from another room, the kind that's ripped from the soul, and she leaned her head back, tightly pressing her eyes shut. But when she opened them again, she was still there. The voices and sobs filled her ears as before.

Uniformed and plain-clothed officers alike walked in and out, going up the stairs and down, plastic gloves on their hands.

She saw Phillips descend and drew away from the wall, walking toward him.

"Everything's under control," he said, catching her arm, his eyes watching her closely. "Evidence technicians are going through his room with a fine-toothed comb. They found a hole in his closet wall the size of a football. He had some shelves pulled in front to hide it. There was a box, Maggie, filled with more pictures of children and with magazines. Pornographic shit the kid shouldn't have been able to get his hands on."

He drew in a breath, his face pale. "He had some computer-generated stuff that would've made a sailor blush. Rameriz said it looks like he'd hooked into some on-line system where you can download some pretty heavy crap. Smut for all tastes and sizes." A blush spread upwards from his collar, and he paused, drawing in a deep breath. "I mean, you think your kid's all right, that he's safe and sound in his room doing homework."

She swallowed, saying nothing.

He dropped his hand from her arm and ran it over his head. "They got the roll of film from his camera. We'll get it developed ASAP. They're taking his dirtbike to the crime lab, but they've dusted it already. Found some smaller prints that could be a child's. There were also a few cotton fibers caught in the stitching on the seat. I'd bet they come up a match with Carrie Spencer's purple overalls. Anyway, we'll know soon enough."

233

It was what she'd expected. Tyler wouldn't have been thinking of clothing fibers and fingerprints. He'd had an impulse, and he went with it.

Only Carrie hadn't wanted to play along.

She'd fought him, and she'd ended up dead, no matter that Tyler had claimed it was an accident.

He had taken her life, and now he'd taken his own.

An eye for an eye, isn't that how it went?

But Maggie didn't feel any great sense of justice.

A boy who'd been molested had grown up to molest and to kill. That was the pattern, wasn't it? Abuse begat abuse like a circle that went on forever.

Until someone stopped it.

One way or another.

She looked past Phillips at the slow parade moving in and out of the house. "He was just a kid," she whispered, her mouth too dry to say more. She wet her lips. "He was so confused. So bitter."

"He killed someone, Maggie," Phillips said, as if she'd forgotten somehow. "He killed a little girl."

"I know." She'd told him what Tyler had said in the few minutes before he'd turned the shotgun on himself, and she couldn't shake the sound of his voice, his torment. The sense that somehow he'd lost himself through no fault of his own.

"He wasn't right up here," Phillips said, tapping a finger to his brow. "Don't tell me it wasn't his fault, okay? Like those twenty-something brats gunned down their parents in Beverly Hills. Blame somebody else, that's the motto for their generation."

Maggie knew what he was talking about, and there was

234

no excuse for what Tyler had done. But there was a reason.

"What he went through with his grandfather, the abuse—it can twist you in so many ways, and if you're not strong enough, if you can't find some way to fight it, and no one's there to save you...."

She couldn't finish.

"Hey, Ryan, you all right?"

She tried to smile, to reassure him as she always had everyone. But it didn't work.

She pushed her purse strap higher on her shoulder and reached for his hand, briefly clasping it.

"I will be," she told him, before she headed to the door and escaped.

Maggie gave her statement at the station, telling everything she'd seen and heard as the video camera watched from the corner of the ceiling. She waited until her every word had been transcribed onto paper, and then she signed it, her hand still shaking.

She didn't stick around afterward, merely long enough to make a phone call. Then she took off again.

She drove across Litchfield to an undeveloped pasture on the edge of town, one she'd passed time and again. The fenced-in property had a pond in its midst and grazing cows that ventured out when the day was warm enough.

She parked the car, leaving her keys inside, and walked through the dried grass, brown stalks crunching underfoot. She got a leg over the wooden post and drew herself up onto the fence, sitting there, catching the heels of her loafers on the rail beneath, looking at the cows who moved as if they were walking in their sleep. Seeing the vague ripple of the water in the pond, the breeze hardly more than a weak breath against her cheek.

Between scudding clouds, the sun made an occasional appearance, and Maggie tilted her face up to its warmth.

If only for a moment, the tiniest bit of peace settled over her, but it was gone as swiftly as the sun was swept behind a cloud.

Then her head filled again with thoughts of the Spencers and the Vincents, and she wondered how long their nightmares would go on. She knew their lives had been forever changed, regardless.

She heard the approaching hum of a motor, the crackle of tires on gravel, and turned her head to see a dust-covered silver sedan pull up on the shoulder.

The car door slammed, and Terry walked up, her dark hair streaked with red beneath the sun, her camel-hair coat unbuttoned.

She stepped across the patchy ground in her sensible pumps, coming up beside Maggie. She rested her arms on the fence. "I feel like I should hum 'Old MacDonald's Farm,'" she said. "You come here often?"

Maggie smiled. "Only when I need to think."

"I'm glad you called me."

"I hope I didn't pull you out of a session..."

"It's okay." Terry reached for her hand and squeezed. "You said you needed to talk about something. The boy you mentioned?"

Maggie looked away. "This isn't easy."

"It never is," Terry said softly, letting go of her hand, standing beside her quietly until Maggie found the strength to speak.

"I understood him," she whispered. "I don't mean about why he killed Carrie Spencer, but about his abuse. He was talking about me, too." Her chest tightened, but she couldn't stop now that she'd started. "He felt betrayed because no one had stopped it. No one had come to his rescue." She gazed out across the pasture, feeling things begin to shake loose inside her; things she'd worked for years to push back into the darkest corners of her head. "I always thought my mother would protect me, that nothing bad would ever happen. But it did...for eight years."

Tears filled her eyes, slipping down her cheeks. Clumsily, she brushed at them. "I thought I deserved it, that I was being punished because my father left."

"You thought that was your fault? So you blamed yourself?"

Maggie got out a strangled, "Yes."

"You figured you deserved it?"

"I don't know." She pressed her eyes closed, seeing her stepfather's face, breathing in the smells of him, until she thought she would choke. "I was five when he started. When it stopped, I was thirteen."

Terry leaned her head against Maggie's arm. "Listen to me," she said softly. "You were a child. You didn't do anything. No one invites abuse, and in your brain, you know it, too. It's just your heart that's having trouble sorting out what really happened. You wanted to be protected, and no one protected you."

"I just want to forget," she said, shivering, and Terry's arm came around her. She couldn't do it anymore. She couldn't keep pretending everything was in order, that she was all right.

"Have you ever tried to talk to your mother?

"No." She avoided Terry's eyes.

"You think she knew, though, don't you?"

Maggie didn't answer. She couldn't.

But Terry read her anyhow.

"Oh, God, Mag, I'm sorry."

Terry's hand slipped over hers, and Maggie whispered, "So am I."